Hadrosaur Tales
Volume XV

Hadrosaur Tales
Volume XV

Edited by David Lee Summers
Published by William Grother

Hadrosaur Productions
Las Cruces, NM

Hadrosaur Tales
Volume Fifteen

All Rights Reserved

Copyright © 2002 by Hadrosaur Productions

Cover Art by Marcia Borell

ISBN # 1-885093-28-4

Printed in the United States by Morris Publishing
3212 East Highway 30
Kearney, NE 68847
1-800-650-7888

The Future Is Now

George Santayana said, "Those who cannot remember the past are condemned to repeat it." I would offer that this proposition could be pointed in the other direction as well: those who cannot see the future are condemning others to repeat the past.

What am I getting at?

One of the misconceptions of those outside the science fiction community is that somehow science fiction predicts, or enlightens us to, future events. It comes up with glimpses of technology or society which many find totally alien. This works its way into popular culture and is the genesis behind some of the science fiction we see in the popular media of television and movies. The perfect example of this is how *Star Trek* "predicted" things like cell phones, floppy disks, and medical imaging technology.

While those technologies bear a striking resemblance to technology we now take for granted, it was hardly a predictor of things to come. The fact is the roots of those technologies were just coming to the fore in the late 60's and early 70's. Through the relentless pace of scientific discovery they became reality in the 80's and 90's. In this new Millennium, we find it hard to imagine a time before CAT scans, MRI, pagers, cell phones, and wireless Internet.

Literary science fiction has never gone in for predicting things. Classic science fiction deals more in the grand scale than the micro scale of individual technologies. Read *Foundation* today, and you read a re-telling of the fall of the Roman Empire; the story is still as relevant today as it was in the 50's when it was published. Never mind that there is no mention of computers; at the time *Foundation* was written, they were still room-sized hulks of vacuum tubes. Your mind (as my mind did) filled them in later on as they started to become more ubiquitous, sitting on our desktops and entering our offices.

Even before Los Alamos and The Manhattan Project, some science fiction writers had picked up on the ideas coming out of Europe and America in the field of physics and envisioned nuclear power. Robert Heinlein may not have anticipated exactly how America would get to the Moon in the late 60's, but his stories were filled with plausible ideas on the subject and engineers had considered them at one time or another before he had even written them.

Science fiction dances around the edge of prophecy because even the most enlightened and educated writer can only see so much in the past and present that can be extrapolated into the future. While many writers knew of computers in the 50's and wrote stories about them, they did not foresee the breakthroughs in metallurgy and miniaturization that would allow the creation of billions of transistors on wafers of silicon. A science fiction writer can only do so much research and cannot afford to saddle a story with long explanations of metallurgy, quantum physics, or cosmology to make a point. The writer has to hope the reader has enough general knowledge to accept the premises that may be written into a story to make it work.

And lets face it, science fiction takes lots of liberties. Its safe to say we are not on the verge of developing warp drive, hyperdrive, wormhole creation technology, or matter teleportation in the foreseeable future. Self-aware, functional robots are only now moving from fantasy to reality. Science has a lot further to go before the deeper mysteries of the universe may be explained easily.

If science fiction does not purport to predict the future and we cannot say with any great certainty that the ideas in it are liable to be seen in the immediate future of Mankind, then just what is it that makes it so important?

My answer is simple: it gives us a glimpse of what may come. I don't mean technology; I mean the journey of human society forward in time. Technology, as James Burke has pointed out on numerous occasions, is a double-edged sword. It has allowed us to survive, grow, and flourish, but it has also distanced us from an acknowledgement of the effects that technology is having on our environment and us. In the first episode of his series *Connections*, Burke pointed out that technology is a trap we too easily fall into. It solves all our problems, but then creates new ones that we do not recognize until the technology fails. And when technology fails, we often do not recognize the potential peril we are in.

So science fiction's job, if I may be permitted, is to show us the future as it may be. It gives us a glimpse of how human nature, the way we are now as a society and a civilization, will affect our future as we move into it. It points out that human nature being what it is, technology will make some societal problems go away, while opening up new avenues for our suspicion, fear, prejudice, and ignorance. It will give some power they did not have before— witness the freedom of speech and thought that the Internet has brought to many people who could not be heard—and others will find the power they already have increased. It will give us opportunities to travel to new places, live on new worlds, and hopefully not pillage them as we have our home planet.

We bring you *Hadrosaur Tales* because we hope the ideas in these stories will entertain you, certainly, but more importantly that they will make you think. Perhaps you will learn something new or be shocked or dismayed—you may even feel compelled to look harder at the world as it is now and your place in it. Whatever occurs, it is my sincere wish that the experience be well worth it, that you enjoy reading the well-written, thought-provoking stories on these pages as much as we enjoy bringing them to you.

So open your mind, let your thoughts settle, and prepare to be transported to the future... first stop, Sheila B. Roark's vision of a *Mystical Realm...*

William Grother
Roselle Park, NJ

CONTENTS

CONTENTS

Mystical Realm

Only dreamers see this land
that's hidden far away
covered by the silver stars
found in the Milky Way.

Unicorns play every day
upon the emerald grass
and nibble on the crystal fruit
that looks as clear as glass.

The quartz lake in the distance
shines brightly in the sun
and tiny fairies preen their wings
until the day is done.

In this special, mystic realm
another sight to see
is horses donned with golden wings
that fly unbound and free.

So, if you want to visit here
just dream your dreams each night
and travel through the silver stars
that glow with spirit light.

— Sheila B. Roark

The Teak Man

By Daniel J. Lesco

Joe Wright thought he was opening his eyes after a deep sleep. He realized several disconcerting things: he couldn't move; he couldn't close his eyes or even change his view by an iota; he apparently was perched on some sort of tiered table covered with huge figurines, lamps, and bookends. His mind swirled while his body remained frozen.

His last memory, slowly crystallizing, was of a massive bald man pointing a large gun in his face, while his wife stood to the side, her face rigid with determination but still beautiful with her elegant nose and her large eyes set back, but not deep-sunk by any means. The man was ordering him aboard the small sailboat—for a convenient nighttime accident, he had suddenly realized. He still loved Laura, but she obviously didn't love him anymore. *Would protest be of any use?* he remembered thinking in desperation. Her last words to him emerged: She loved Thomas but he was in debt and they needed Joe's insurance money to get a new start (hardly—Joe knew the lover as a purported embezzler of investment funds); she knew Joe had his own lover (wrong—just loved himself and his own interests too much.)

He had a vague memory of her paid assassin punching him viciously in the stomach and pushing him over the side, while she cried quietly (probably felt she ought to) and Thomas watched with disdain as the dirty work was done—then water rushing around him, through his nose and mouth, and the awful pain.

He mentally shuddered and turned his attention to his current plight. He couldn't move his head or eyes, but he did have a wide field-of-view, perceiving the entire hemisphere before his... eyes? The first thing that drew his attention was his enormous belly jutting out in a disgusting way, being the only part of his body that he could see other than the vague shadow of his flat nose. And that belly was made of wood.

Joe had a cherished collection of woodcarvings, mostly animals and bizarre figurines from foreign lands. He loved the feel of polished wood and could recognize most of the better carving woods: creamy brown basswoods, dark walnuts, Cuban and Honduran red-brown mahoganies. He thought his belly was carved from teak, yellow-tan and burnished to a waxy luster.

He presumed he was in a shop of some sort. There were more tables and shelves in front of him, all loaded with objects with price tags dangling from bright orange string. On the wall shelf opposite him was a mirrored picture frame in which he could see himself—or rather, the belly that supported the eyes or whatever he looked out through.

Apparently he was now an integral part of a large carving of an ancient Oriental-appearing warrior. He noted his bald head, the loincloth, and the vest pushed open by that massive and solid gut, the sword dangling from one hand, the sullen face. All was carved with fine detail—a beautiful work of carving of a repulsive being. How had he become attached to this evil figure?

He was certain now he had died and that this was some sort of afterlife. But he felt impatient and unsettled, as if he still had unfinished business waiting for him. How long would this state go on? Would he ever know what was happening? Actually, he had been pretty much a devoted agnostic who didn't think there was going to be anything after the brain synapses stopped their tiny sparking.

When Joe heard noises coming from behind his visual perspective, he realized he also retained his sense of hearing, although the sounds seemed to be reaching him as through a long tunnel.

He studied his surroundings in more detail. The other objects on his table were arranged haphazardly as to type or size. He noted a few other carvings, including an Indian mounted on a horse and a rather large eagle. Most of what he could see he considered the junk that interested the less serious antique collectors. What he saw of the shop suggested that it was small, but brightly lit and clean.

* * *

Many days and nights passed by. One day a young boy, perhaps ten, came into the shop and stood in front of him, staring for a lengthy time until his mother came over. The sandy-haired boy asked his mom about buying the neat statue; Joe could tell she was horrified at the prospect of Joe in her house. To the boy, the Oriental warrior was probably symbolic of a protector, rather than the intimidator he would be to anyone mature enough to have read Howard's Conan or appreciated Frazetta's art. Joe found himself wondering what kind of father the boy had to protect him.

The mother was tall and blond with a lush figure, her face a touch drawn and overly made-up. She was very well dressed. Joe wished he could wink at her to see her reaction. But his mere thought of doing so seemed to make the nervous woman flinch. She rushed the boy out of Joe's sight; then he heard the shop's door open and close.

* * *

As the months passed, notable events seldom occurred, although Joe enjoyed studying the shop's patrons who wandered the aisles in front of him. Few actually bought anything.

He occasionally saw the shopkeeper, who ran the shop by himself. When he (rarely) went out to lunch, by himself or with a client or supplier, the shop was closed for the hour or two. The shopkeeper, whose name was Ricardo, kept long hours, often muttered to himself, and seemed to have no real friends or family— so Joe felt that he was a strange character. The encounter with the dope-addict convinced Joe of that.

The entire crisis occurred within Joe's visual field because a customer that day had lifted Joe and set him down again positioned at a right angle to his normal orientation on the table. Ordinarily he didn't face the shop's door or the cash register. The shop was quiet and empty that early evening, just minutes from closing.

The shop had its share of peculiar customers, but this guy looked completely out of place. The thin, longhaired man, dressed in a black raincoat, grabbed the first object he could reach as he entered the shop and held it out to Ricardo, muttering "How much?" Ricardo stood by the cash register, reading a newspaper spread out over the counter. As Ricardo took the large vase from the man with both his hands, a gun appeared in the nervous man's hand, pointed at Ricardo's face.

There were words of caution and urgency. The thief's gun drooped slightly as the shopkeeper reached into the cash drawer. It surprised even Joe to see a grim Ricardo level his own huge gun at the man's chest. Ricardo spoke urgently, "Two things to consider: my gun's bigger and I'd rather die while killing you than let you get out of here able to pull this crap again on some young mother or father who somebody is going to cry for if you panic and shoot them. So put down your gun—now."

The young man's gun started to shake violently, pointing downward; Ricardo slashed his gun savagely across the counter, hitting the man's neck and dropping him instantly. Joe watched Ricardo calmly take the thief's gun from beneath his fallen body and then call the police. Joe saw Ricardo's hand quiver ever so slightly as he poured himself a small glass of liquor while he waited for the police. From then on, Joe held new respect for the shopkeeper and wished he knew more about Ricardo's life and his past.

* * *

Joe gradually worked out where the antique shop was located, using verbal clues and his few, brief glimpses of the shop's windows when customers picked him up for a cursory examination, together with the memory of his life's last few days and the interrupted fall vacation with his wife in Camden. He was in a shop adjacent to the harbor where the large schooners docked in the Maine tourist town. He didn't remember being in this particular shop with his wife the shopping day before she and her lover had murdered him. But references to some of the streets, the restaurants, and some of the other shops convinced him that his soul or mind or whatever had not traveled far since his death. Through some powerful attraction, his psyche had been pulled to this ancient carving, this soul trap.

At first, his gross carved body disgusted him. It was the opposite of the body he had strove to maintain in his middle-aged life. His dedication to low-fat health foods and exercising, which had progressed from a tiring routine to an invigorating activity, had resulted in what he half-jokingly called his *hardbody* when bragging to his wife and friends. But soon he began to take distorted pride in his powerful, almost obscene new appearance. He wished he could flex his meaty arms and roll the sloping shoulders beneath his thick neck. His carved arms and body were meant to be hairless, although his fine features showed a wispy beard and mustache; he suspected he was of Mongol heritage—in the model used by the artist, he hastened to correct himself. He liked to read the expressions of customers who noticed him. He liked to imagine how they would react to him if he were six feet tall and warm flesh instead of sixteen inches of wood. And if any of the beautiful women that came into the shop would be prurient enough to find his strong body attractive. After all, he chided himself, he hadn't been all that successful with his trim body in attracting invitations from those scrumptious women he had regularly encountered in his life as an insurance peddler.

Joe sometimes pondered the age of his antique wooden form. The only time anyone had inquired about this, Ricardo had said, "At least 100 years, perhaps 400. There's an old gypsy tale that goes with it: something to do with a shaman's containment of spirits, but I forget most of it." The half-interested customer had scoffed and returned Joe to his roost.

* * *

His almost-comfortable existence was jarred one morning when his wife (his ex-wife?) Laura came into the shop with her lover and accomplice. How could they have the nerve to visit again where they had murdered him? Why would they take the chance? He wondered if his body had ever been recovered from the Atlantic.

He studied his wife as she passed before him, glancing at his section of the display table. Although her face seemed tense, Laura chatted with Thomas and even smiled once; she was in no great discomfort to be back at the scene of her crime. *I really meant a lot to her*, Joe thought in sarcasm—and regret. Would he take revenge on her and Thomas if he were able? He surprised himself by even making that prospect a question that required thought.

Then they were gone from the shop, having bought nothing.

Joe didn't have much time to dwell on Laura's reappearance and the memories it resurfaced of his past life as a reasonably successful salesman, of his death and this strange state of limbo. The next day, he was purchased.

She was not young, but certainly not what nowadays most would call middle-aged, and attractive in an exotic way that drew the attention of men who were intrigued by unique women. As soon as she saw Joe, she picked him up and called to Ricardo, who was as usual out of Joe's sight.

"You have this marked as $200. Will you take $150?"

Joe heard Ricardo's murmur of agreement and saw her half-smile. Then he was carried to the counter by the door and soon plastic wrapping obscured his vision.

He didn't feel any excitement or regret at leaving the shop, nor was he anxious or curious. He decided that he felt amusement, since he didn't want to admit to having no emotions left at all.

He'd had a poor sense of the passage of time since his awakening in the carving. He merely recognized time markers such as the opening and closing of the shop. The duration of time before he could again see his surroundings was similarly immeasurable and unimportant to him.

When the wrapping was removed, he was set on what he thought was a fireplace mantle, facing a large, well-furnished room. The woman who had purchased him was standing very still before him, with her hand resting on his smooth belly. Joe noticed again her half-smile and decided that it must be an affectation that had become a habit. Then she left the room by way of an open entrance to Joe's right; Joe was relegated to a position of vigilance devoid of any activity or sound with the exception of the muted ticking of a massive wall clock. Several days and nights passed that way.

Joe realized that his wooden state paralleled in many ways his emotionless existence in his (past) life, subdued by a sour outlook which he could seldom shake off and which helped drive his wife away. Joe had been concerned only with his own needs, sharing less and less with Laura. No children had resulted from their rigid marriage. That was a fortunate failing as it turned out, he thought sardonically. He remembered telling himself that having a son or daughter would have changed him for the better—what a delusion!

So while he admitted that he would hate Laura for her weakness, if he were still capable of feeling strong emotions, Joe blamed himself as much as he blamed her for the murder happening at all. Her lover Thomas was almost a non-factor; he was a despicable man whom Joe had checked up on when he had learned of their burgeoning affair and yet had done nothing about until it was too late. Joe had made no attempt to resolve his problems with Laura and had rejected her hesitant efforts at bridging the widening gap that had separated almost every aspect of their life together.

* * *

Late that evening, the room lights were turned on as his new owner came to stand before Joe on his mantle. She was accompanied by someone whom Joe recognized instantly despite his hazy images of the man—he was the killer that Laura had hired to dispose of her unwanted husband.

"You're a nutcase, Sophia," the big man said, "but I can see why you bought it. Handsome chap."

"I connected you with him the instant I saw his eyes and belly, Jason."

"I've got to get going," Jason said, "I'm getting that boy tonight and I'm bringing him here; so I want you to leave and stay away until I call you. Get a room at the Hilton. Understand? I'm nervous about this one, but it's big money."

She just nodded, her eyes narrowed and piercing. Jason left the room; Sophia stood looking at Joe for a few minutes. Joe did not find anything to be liked in either of the two. The room darkened, leaving Joe to his timeless thoughts.

* * *

Joe heard the sobbing before the lights in the room illuminated the small figure Jason carried. The child had a black hood over his head; his arms were tied loosely behind his back. Jason wore a Halloween mask of a clown.

"It won't do you any good to cry, boy," Jason told him as he set the boy onto a couch in front of Joe. "I won't hurt you. You'll be back home in a day or two, once your parents pay us. I'm going to lock you in a bathroom, so you can take care of yourself. You'll be able to take the hood off. And I'll get you some food later."

The boy continued to cry quietly. Joe knew he must be petrified with fear. Jason talked to the child as if he were a fellow player in the dark world that Jason roamed to make his living. Joe felt the rage building within his wooden body. For the first time since his awakening, his incapacity to do anything besides passively observe the events around him distressed Joe.

Jason untied the boy's arms and then carried him out of the room, returning alone with his mask off after what Joe surmised was a short time. He sank his heavy body onto the couch and picked up a telephone. Joe noted that Jason's expression never changed and wondered what events in Jason's life had submerged his humanity so deep. Sophia was correct that Joe's teak warrior and Jason had much in common.

Joe could decipher from Jason's brief phone call most of the kidnapping plan. Someone who knew the boy's father and his unscrupulous business dealings was paying Jason half the ransom. They hoped to get a million dollars, but would settle for half that. The scheme combined kidnapping and blackmail. In that way, Jason and his accomplice hoped to keep the police from being notified. The other kidnapper was negotiating with the family while Jason hid the child. They would not kill the boy, whose name was Gary, unless he could identify one of them. Joe seethed as he listened to the ruthless plotting. After the call, Jason dozed on the couch.

Several times that night and the next day Jason received phone calls from his accomplice. Joe could tell that things were not going smoothly with the kidnapping plan. Once, Jason slammed the receiver down onto the phone after furiously warning his accomplice that if he didn't straighten things out soon Jason might have to consider him permanently dispensable and would go to great lengths to make his disposal extremely painful.

Joe saw or heard nothing of the boy during this time, but did notice Jason carrying food through the room several times.

The following night, Joe watched the kidnapping plan disintegrate. He was only momentarily surprised when he saw who accompanied Jason into the room—it was Laura's Thomas.

"We've got to cut and run, Jason. Cochran had the police informed all along. I think you're safe for now, but they're onto me."

Jason fumed, "You're a complete fuck-up—I should kill you, too."

"I'll take the boy and dump him in the middle of town

somewhere. Maybe it'll pacify them for a while and I can get a flight out of Boston before they trace me. Laura will have to fend for herself. This is going to get them to reinvestigate her husband's case—I just know it." Thomas ran his hands through his hair in distress. "Where is the boy? I'll get him out of here."

"In the bathroom down the hall."

Thomas returned to the room dragging the boy. Now Joe was truly surprised when he saw the young face: it was the boy who had wanted to buy him in the antique shop. Gary started to cry again and Jason slapped his face. Joe mentally flinched.

"Where's his hood, you fool?" Jason shouted at Thomas. "Now he's seen my face and this room. Do you think I can let him live now?"

Thomas paled. "Look, you can't kill him. He's just a young boy."

Jason pointed his gun at Thomas. "Leave now or I'll kill you too."

Thomas stumbled in his haste to get away from the crazed man, knowing Jason would have no qualms about shooting him. The boy stood terrified.

After his seemingly endless frozen existence, Joe was aware of the fact that he could shift his visual field of view; he could now look to either side of his perch on the mantle. He watched in fury as Jason carried Gary from the room. When he heard the boy cry out, Joe felt the very fibers of his body protest and then things happened in a rush. With a determined effort, he leapt off the mantle. The room seemed to be shrinking, but he realized that he was actually growing rapidly as he fell.

For an instant, he sensed strange thoughts, not his own, a cursory bond with others who had seemingly occupied this bizarre body in ancient times. His vision blurred as he saw, superimposed on the plush room, scenes outside his own past experiences: a low-ceilinged, dark stone room filled with tavern tables, empty of people but for a lone woman who was crudely dressed and obviously pregnant, staring at him with a frozen half-smile; a glimpse of a vast steppe across which scores of men on horses were racing amidst billowing dust. There was an aura of purpose, determination, will—

he wasn't certain what to call it since his life had been devoid of such drive for so many years.

The ghostly images vanished; he felt as if mental and physical shackles had been removed. Joe was in complete control of his new body that towered almost to the ceiling. He was still wooden, but of wood alive with power. He saw that his sword was razor sharp and trusted its hardwood strength as if it were Damascus steel.

Joe remembered Ricardo's fearlessness—not born of stupidity, he knew now, but bravery—with the thief in his shop. Joe had nothing to lose, nothing to fear. Life was sometimes violent, but now Joe seemed to be accumulating violence.

He found Jason covering Gary's face with a pillow in an adjacent bedroom. A ferocious grunt emerged from his throat, although his lips did not open. Jason turned and Joe saw a reaction in his dead eyes for the first time. Disbelief was followed by the first tinge of fear as he backed away from Gary and pulled his gun from under his coat. Joe's rage and power fed each other; he clenched Jason's shoulder and lifted him completely off the floor. Jason fired his gun point-blank at Joe. Joe knew one bullet struck his belly and another splintered his cheek, but they had no effect on him.

Despite his rage, Joe almost felt calm as he swung his sword and Jason's head flew unencumbered into the bedroom wall and fell behind the bed. Joe turned to look at Gary, who was staring in disbelief at the monstrous wooden warrior. Joe wanted to comfort the boy, tell him that the terror was over. Then the room was growing before Joe's eyes and he was once again a rigid, sixteen-inch warrior. As he watched the boy, relief overwhelmed Joe and his eyes seemed to dim with mist.

Gary knew enough to call 911.

* * *

The boy held the teak warrior in his hands and looked at his mother. "Look at the scars from the bullets, Mom; they're hardly noticeable. I'll call him Batu. Batu will always protect me." She just nodded, wondering if anyone would ever be able to explain what had happened in that bedroom and why her son was capable of holding up so well in the face of the unbelievable carnage. She was not able to let go of her son for an instant, afraid he would be overcome with shock. Joe did not see or hear any of this exchange. He was gone.

sweet

the grass must grow
green and tall
our children
wither and die

— Geoff Sawers

the park-keepers threaten another strike

They only go out to mow the grass
in pairs now
they say the moles round here are the size
of bears now

— Geoff Sawers

THE POWER OF THE MIND

By M. L. Archer

With naked arms and legs Charlotte gripped her beloved husband even closer to her and pulled, pulled at him. "Maybe this time will do it," she whispered to him. "Wayne, Wayne, let's make it this time!" For their whole two years of blissful marriage hadn't they longed so for a pregnancy? She didn't want to give up and go the route of fertility tests, taking temperatures before lovemaking or any of the other garbage she'd heard of from Marilyn and Cleo. But her fantasies might maximize her chances, the fantasies she had been indulging in lately, of the splendid, great chestnut horse towering over her, his dong, long, immense and blackish except at the whitish tip, and with it dripping semen, drop after huge drop into her openness, eager to receive it. Only lately, since she had worked at the regional office of the Endangered Species Act had that horse taken over her mind at times like this, the frequent, wonderful times. What harm was there in sexual fantasies? All the marriage manuals she had studied, both alone and with Wayne, had said how fantasization helped sexual function and enjoyment. Of course they'd meant fantasizing about other people, not horses, but what the heck? The fantasies were harmless.

Wayne kissed her neck and plunged himself inside her. Again and again he plunged inside her and in her minds-eye the horse plunged and dripped into her. Drip, drip, drip, drip. "Oh darling, I love you so," Wayne said.

"And I love you too," she answered and she gripped harder on his naked torso. The horse never neighed, just raced to her in silence and dripped and plunged into her. And ultimately sprayed her with a great gush of liquid which she pulled, pulled, pulled into herself. Wayne gushed into her and the horse did too.

Oh, fantasizing was so lovely. Her body sucked, sucked Wayne's and the horse's thick semen into herself. Into herself!

Two weeks later, with happiness a shout in her, she went for a pregnancy test. She was going to have a baby! She knew she was! *Positive*, the report said. Oh, it was positive!

As Wayne, with his briefcase in one hand and a denim-gray suit on him looking too sedate for the day, opened the door that dusk, she, home before him, raced against him. "Oh Wayne," she said and she snuggled against him and she repeated what she'd told him on the phone. "It was definitely positive. We are! We are!"

His face crumpled with happiness and his hand flung away the briefcase and he squeezed her to him. Wordlessly he nodded again and again and he kissed her cheeks, her hair, her eyebrows, her neck, her lips and he kissed her tears of happiness away and her fingers stroked the tears from his cheeks.

At a celebrative dinner at Le Mácconaiss, he said, "Have the grilled salmon, Sweetie, and not the Caesar salad. The salad still might have pesticide residues on it." He tilted his handsome head to one side and smiled at her. "I suppose now's the time for you to be quitting your job?"

"Quitting?" They'd never discussed that. Would he quit his briefs for toxic spill prosecutions, just because of a pregnancy? "I'm only pregnant a few weeks. No, I think I'll not quit yet. The work's too important. Oh, I think towards the end, or if I have any trouble carrying, I must, but not just yet. Though I'm only a diminutive cog in the mechanism there, my work's important. We can't let all the beautiful and wondrous animals vanish from the earth." She hesitated and the horse flashed across her mind. "But if the doctor advises me to quit, I certainly will." There must be nothing to endanger this baby. But Mother had said to her, "I worked up to a month before I delivered you." and her best friend, Brenda, had worked up to the last week and nothing had happened to herself or to Brenda's son.

"I know how you love animals." He laid the warmth of his huge hand over hers on the tablecloth. "And want to save them. But there are other things too. And saving them doesn't really depend on you. Shortly you can be home caring for our baby and so—" He hesitated. "—so you could buy that horse you've always wanted. We can build that stable you've wanted. You wouldn't even have to board the horse out. We could hire some young man to help with it. Quitting work, you could get even closer to animals."

Her eyes shone. "Oh darling, could we?" She clutched his hand with the wedding ring on it that she had given him. What a good, thoughtful husband he was. And enticing. The muscles in his arms had entranced her when she'd first met him on the Williams' tennis court and she'd been astonished to learn he was a law student and not an athlete. "I work out every day," he had said and his blue eyes had said something else, something rousing, to her. They had bought this house on its fourteen acres, on the edge of fashionable Los Altos Hills so their children—when they came— would have room to roam, so eventually the children could have rabbits and maybe a goat and she could buy a horse and someday they too would have their own horses. "No," she reflected aloud, "I'll not buy a horse yet. Let's wait awhile and see how this pregnancy goes." Now why had she said that? She didn't know why. Hadn't she always yearned, yearned for a horse, a lovely chestnut horse, light on its feet and with its sculptured head poised proudly high. "There's plenty of time to do that, after our baby is born."

She was not sick to her stomach and did not suffer many other symptoms, though she quickly grew pretty large. And she and Wayne spent their hours together in happiness.

She went for her ultrasound. In eagerness she watched the screen. The shape of a colt came up on the screen. She stifled her scream with both her hands. A colt! How could that be? A colt! The fantasy!

But the doctor seemed not to notice what showed clearly on the screen. "Everything looks normal, Mrs. Grayson," he said. "It's a male. And everything looks as if you will have no problem."

Oh my God! No problems!

On the drive back to the office, her mind raced. The fantasy, the fantasy, and now she was fantasizing a colt in her stomach! She must never fantasize again! The fantasies were turning into craziness.

Back at home with her mind a turmoil she cooked a dinner of chicken in tarragon sauce and she tore lettuce and sliced radishes and diced up tomatoes for a salad. Was chicken good for a colt? She must eat more greens, more grass. No, she had never eaten grass.

This was a baby, not a colt. She must stop this fantasizing. Stop it! "A male," she told Wayne, who'd been out of his office when she'd phoned earlier. "The doctor says everything looks normal."

At work she read over the long, long list of endangered animals. Chestnut horses were not on the list. No, get your mind away from horses, she warned herself.

The list engraved itself on her mind.

Her pregnancy continued—with no unusual medical problems. Sometimes she felt the tiny hooves beating on her, the pulse of the heart of the colt. She quit work. She could not concentrate on that list of endangered animals with this colt—baby—growing in her. She swelled larger.

She's planned to make baby clothes, but she made none and only reluctantly helped purchase them, when Wayne happily selected this and that. "It might be bad luck to buy a crib and a bassinet now," she said to him in the midst of the baby furniture at Baby Wonderland. "Maybe we shouldn't anticipate too much."

"Oh, horse balls!" he exclaimed with the happiness in his voice. "I want to anticipate every minute of it. This year I don't believe in bad luck."

"I must go home for the delivery," she suddenly announced to him at breakfast one morning. She couldn't give birth to a colt here; Wayne would be shocked; he might even instantly renounce his love for her and divorce her; the doctors would be disgraced.

"But why, darling?" he asked with his blue eyes troubled. "Here, you have me. It's too far away. I thought you never truly cared if you ever saw the area around Chihuahua again. Your mother can drop her oil paints for a few weeks and come here."

"No, I must go there! Or near there!" Thank the planet Jupiter that Wayne had dozens of cases coming up in the courts and could not lay off work to go so far away, for so long. She would live not with Mother, but at the lovely house and stables north of there, where she had learned to ride and had learned to love horses. "Mother wrote that my room's now her studio. So I'll live with Rob and Sarah. Remember the people who owned a stable? They've always wanted me to come down for a vacation. This won't be a vacation, but they'll welcome me just the same." She could take them into her confidence, but they would be shocked. But they would never tell Wayne anything. After all they hardly knew Wayne. Had seen him only twice. But they'd assisted mares in strings of births of colts.

"I don't like the idea at all." Wayne's eyes looked as troubled as the least reassurable of his lawyers on one of their most dicey days. "But of course—if the doctor says its okay—pregnant wives have to be indulged." He firmed his lips and thought a second. "I'll come down for the birth anyway. I wouldn't miss it for anything in the world! And I won't care what's on the calendar!"

Her thoughts clenched. She had never lied to him before this colt. "The doctor thinks it's going to be late," she said. "The head hasn't even begun to travel downward yet." Wasn't that really what happened, even with a colt? She gave him a late, late date. God would forgive her; poor Wayne somehow must be protected from ever knowing. Or, perhaps, he would blame himself. Perhaps he would even get mentally ill over it. No! That was it; she was mentally ill, as some papers, which she'd read, had stated a few pregnant women sometimes temporarily became.

At the San Francisco Airport, she flew southward and moved in with Rod and Sarah and told them the situation and saw them search each other's eyes for clues as to what to think. "I'm telling you the truth," she said. "Please don't say anything to anyone we know. At least wait and see!"

The sizable unwillingness still busied itself in their eyes, their desire to rush out and tell someone, "Charlotte's crazy, poor thing! Crazy!"

"It's only for a little while," she said. "Then, if I'm wrong, you can have me hauled away to the bobby hatch."

She talked their reluctance into at least waiting. She said nothing of the colt to Mother. Mother lived her own busy life and had but scant time for her.

In clean straw in a stall in the stable, she gave birth to the baby and it was a colt as she'd known it would be, a chestnut colt, wobbly on its long legs, but with a royally-shapely head. It would be a stunningly beautiful horse someday, just like the horse which had raced to her as she'd lain in Wayne's arms and which had sprayed its semen into her. She hugged the colt to her. Her colt! Her very own colt!

"The baby was born early… and stillborn," she told Wayne over the phone and even at their distance from each other she and he mingled their sobs. "No, there's no use your coming down."

"To compensate I'm going to buy that horse you mentioned," eventually she said. "No—please—I said there's no use at all your leaving your cases and flying down. Mother, Rod, Sarah and myself will tend to everything here. Throwing yourself into your work will help you." Rod had even made a small casket for her and them and Mother to bury, though here in this spot in this land there was no need for the formalities and legalities of The States. And, if any problems popped up, money could grease a few palms. Why couldn't she have had a baby and a colt too? "It will take a little while for me to select one and to buy a car and a trailer," she added.

"Sweetheart, are you all right?" he asked with the pain for the lost baby and for her in his voice. "That's the most important consideration."

"Nor quite yet," she answered. "But I will be by the time I get home." Over the line, she could almost feel the pain in him. "It's not the end of the world. Shortly we can try for another baby."

Almost wordlessly, Rod and Sarah bought a horse trailer for her and went with her while she bought a car and hired a driver to drive horse, trailer and car north to the border. Rod and Sarah asked her nothing of how the colt had happened and of what she had told Wayne. Now and then, they merely stared at each other with an extremity of puzzlement in their eyes.

The happiness ballooned in her as she sat beside Juan, with Lustrous, the colt, in the trailer behind her and the miles northward spinning away to behind them. How could Wayne not be joyful over Lust? He was so beautiful? So alive. They were young. Plenty of time to have a real baby. Or two or three even.

At the border, Juan turned the car over to her. "Muchas gracias," she said. He would return to his home from here. "I'm sure I can make it from here with no trouble."

When she pulled into the driveway, Wayne's Toyota was parked in it.

The door opened and he ran toward the car and she leaped out and sprinted to him and they hugged and kissed and again tears raced down his face. "Oh darling," he said, "to go through all that alone. I wish you'd let me be there with you every minute. Or at least for the birth. I had sworn I'd be there, you know."

She opened the door of the trailer and set up the ramp and she led Lust out. He stared at it in amazement. "Why he's beautiful!" he exclaimed. "I had no idea a colt could be so beautiful."

She nodded. She led Lust to the stable which Wayne, utilizing Rod's phone advice, had had built three hundred yards behind the house. She could hardly wait to get into Wayne's arms again. And he could hardly wait to get her into his arms again in bed she could tell. So many animals were endangered; she could fantasize a wolf, though wolves were coming back nicely, a black rhino, a Bengal tiger, a snow leopard, an elephant, but an elephant had to be carried so many months. Twice—she vowed—I will fantasize a real baby, so Wayne will be happy too. Maybe someday she could even take him into her confidence. She would never return to her work. In bed, she would just use the power of her mind.

White to Pink

The little White Rose Princess
was lonely every day
and hoped to find her one true love
to chase her blues away.

Every night beneath the stars
she dreamed about her knight,
a prince to give her all his love
and make her future bright.

She'd fold her velvet petals
and prayed with all her might
that he would find her standing there
filled with love's golden light.

One day he finally came to her
and filled her heart with glee
that's when the little Princess Rose
turned pink as she could be.

In her magic land of dreams
a long, long time ago,
a white rose turned a blushing pink
and shined with loving glow.

That's why we have pink roses
that's why our gardens glow
because a princess fell in love
a long, long time ago.

— Sheila B. Roark

MINDSWITCH

By Donald Sullivan

I wrestled the pickup over the rough dirt road winding through Blackroot State Forest. Seeing a clearing ahead that was suitable to park the pickup, I pulled over and killed the engine. I stepped out of the pickup, stretched, and drew in a deep breath of the cool, crisp autumn air. It felt good to be in the woods again.

After strapping on my ivory-handled hunting knife, I pulled my Army surplus carbine from the rack and set out on foot into the woods.

As I made my way through the woods, my eye caught a movement overhead. Looking up through the openings between branches, I caught a glimpse of a glowing egg-shaped object soaring by overhead. UFO was the first thing that popped into my mind, though I had never believed in the things. I immediately dismissed the thought, figuring that it was a weather balloon or some such and continued hiking through the woods.

I'm no great hunter… not even a good hunter. Some say that my choice of hunting weapons proves that. But I go into the woods often during the hunting season, using hunting as an excuse to enjoy the cool, bracing autumn season when the woods are free of bugs and snakes.

Again, I saw a movement overhead and looked up to see the egg-shaped object hovering directly overhead. I stared at it. Plainly, it wasn't a weather balloon; I guessed that I was seeing some kind of U.S. Air Force experimental aircraft.

Suddenly, the object began descending, and in a matter of seconds it was only a hundred feet overhead. The object was fairly large, perhaps seventy or eighty feet in length. A hatch in the belly of the craft slid open, and a figure came floating down toward me.

I remember thinking that I'd stumbled into an off-limits area, and the air force was coming to chase me out. The figure floated down and landed about ten feet in front of me. Astonished, I refused to believe what I was seeing with my own eyes. Maybe the Air Force was playing some kind of joke, I thought, but immediately discarded the idea.

What I was seeing was no joke. It was real. I was seeing a creature about seven feet tall. Its face could have been a cross between a human and a lizard, and its scaly skin was rusty red. It wore silver coveralls, boots, and a wide studded belt.

Somewhere in the back of my mind, something was telling me that this wasn't really happening to me. This was impossible. This wasn't reality. But when I recovered from my shock enough to notice that its hand was doing something with the belt, I became aware that this was for real—and the thing was going for a weapon.

I immediately raised my carbine in self-defense, but as I did so, the creature abruptly became a man. The man looked familiar, and he was pointing a carbine at me. Again, my mind was questioning the reality of the situation, for the man I was looking at could be my identical twin.

The man spoke. "You are looking at yourself, Jack Ramsey. We have switched bodies, or to be more precise, we have switched minds. Look at your body.

I looked down to see the silver coveralls the thing had worn, and then looked at the scaly rust-red skin on my hands. I cried out in anguish, but my voice was not there; it was replaced with a hoarse growl.

Anger began to well up inside me—my fear and shock was turning to outrage. I bellowed in the hoarse growl and took a step toward him.

He trained the carbine on my chest. "Take another step and I will kill you," he said. "Also, I remind you that if you attack me you attack your own body. The body you now possess is superior in strength to your own body, and you could easily kill me with your bare hands. But if you kill me, you will be forever trapped in the body you now possess. You would be a freak among your own kind."

Still outraged, I had the irrational urge to attack him and take my body back by force. But I recovered enough to see the logic of what he had said.

"Who are you?" I managed in the hoarse growl that was now my voice. "How do you know my name? Why are you doing this?"

"I am called Drugor," he said, "and I am of the Jhinn, the most powerful race in the galaxy. I know your name, and your language, because I am skilled in the practice of mind exchange. My mind now occupies your body, including your brain. I delve into your brain and extract the information I need."

Logic told me that if this creature now inhabiting my body could read my brain, it followed that I should be able to read his brain as well. He seemed to know what I was thinking.

"It takes many years of training and experience to develop the skills that I have acquired. Mind exchange involves only the exchange of the conscious level of the mind. Your brain retains all your memories on the subconscious level, allowing me to tap those memories. In a matter of moments I knew your entire past.

"As time passes," Drugor went on, "you will find that you will be able to tap into the subconscious level of my brain—but to a much lesser degree. Without proper training, however, you will be very limited on what you can learn."

Drugor kept the carbine trained on my chest. "Remove the belt from around your waist," he commanded.

I followed his instructions and handed the belt to him. He backed away for a distance, leaned the carbine against a tree, and donned the belt. He had to make adjustments to make the belt fit his small human body; my body is only five-feet-nine at a hundred sixty pounds.

After the belt was adjusted, Drugor keyed several studs on the belt as if he were tapping out a code. My weight seemed to leave me, and I felt a force pulling me upward. The two of us were drawn into the ship, and a hatch sealed shut behind us.

He led me through the airlock and into a compartment. He seated me at a table and then seated himself across from me, obviously satisfied that I wasn't going to make any trouble.

"I am going down to have a look at your world," he said. "I will explore the region from which you come and return to the ship in two or three of your days. You will remain on the ship.

"As the subconscious memories of my brain come to your mind—and that will happen—you will learn your way around the ship. You may even learn to operate the ship, but it will do you no good. I have neutralized all the ship's controls. The ship can now be operated only from the remote controls on my belt.

"When I leave the ship, it is programmed to ascend to a point beyond detection of your people's instruments, where it will remain until I recall it. I advise you to be patient and to do nothing foolish while I am away."

With that, the Jhinn departed, and I found myself alone on an alien ship. I walked over to a porthole and looked out. I was astonished to see that I was already so far from Earth that it looked like a big blue and white globe.

I looked around the compartment I now occupied. As I inspected the equipment in the compartment, some of Drugor's memories began to surface. As Drugor had predicted, his memories were beginning to supply me with information about the ship.

It was almost as if our minds were merging together. Not only was I remembering information about the ship, but I was also recalling things about his past. I felt as if I were actually experiencing parts of his life. Drugor had predicted that I would be unable to tap into his subconscious memories at will, and this was certainly true. But I knew that I was getting more from his mind than he figured I would. I had no way of knowing why this was so, but I reasoned that there was an X-factor in the human psyche—unknown to the Jhinn—that enabled me to dig deeper into Drugor's mind than the Jhinn thought possible.

The equipment in the compartment, I learned, was for exercise and recreation. I even found the Jhinn equivalent of movies and video games. In Drugor's part of my mind, I understood the games, but to my own mind the games made no sense. I left the rec room.

As I explored the ship, a feeling of déjà vu came over me. I knew the ship as well as Drugor, I supposed. I even knew how to operate the ship; it was fairly simple, even to my human mind. But Drugor was right: he had nullified the controls on the ship, and only the controls on his belt could operate the ship now. I knew that I could also operate the controls on the belt—if I only had the belt. But Drugor had the belt and control of the ship, and he was on Earth below doing God-knows-what.

I began to worry about him. Suppose he had an accident. Or got arrested. Or got mugged. I would be forever stranded on this ship, and even if I could figure out a way to override the belt controls, I would be stuck in this freakish body forever.

As I moved around the ship, I found the control room, the sleeping quarters, and the galley. In the galley, I checked the menu and found some of Drugor's favorite meals. I keyed the menu and the meal was served. I found the Jhinn meal delicious, but suspected that my human palate would have found it disgusting.

My stomach now full, I felt tired and sleepy. I made my way to the sleeping quarters and lay down on Drugor's bed. The bed was comfortable to my Jhinn body, but I was unable to sleep.

As I lay there, several questions entered my mind. Who were the Jhinn? Why was Drugor here? What was he doing on Earth below? As if responding to my queries, the answers began to flow from Drugor's subconscious mind.

The Jhinn considered themselves as masters of the galaxy. It was their destiny to conquer and rule over every planet in the galaxy. They had already conquered many planets, but were constantly searching for more. Thousands of scouts, such as Drugor, were sent out in search of new worlds.

Upon finding a world, scouts were instructed to note the location, make a cursory exploration, and then transmit a report to the Jhinn High Command, who would lay plans for the invasion.

A Jhinn scout considered the mind exchanger as his most important tool. It was built into the scout's utility belt, and all scouts were required to be experts in using the device. After an exchange, a scout must do two things: He must recover his belt immediately after the exchange and he must take every precaution to protect his body after the exchange.

I now realized that I was not being held prisoner to prevent my escape, but I was being held to prevent Drugor's body from coming to harm. Drugor had chosen the best possible place to leave his body— a Jhinn ship.

But if Drugor was so concerned with the safety of his body, why had he threatened me with the carbine to regain the utility belt? After all, he was pointing the weapon at his own body. Again, the answer came from Drugor's subconscious mind.

Drugor's body was shielded. A thin protective undersuit instantly hardened upon impact from a sudden blow. Drugor's body was never in danger. But I also learned that the most vulnerable part of a Jhinn's body was a spot just below the chest—about where the human navel would be.

There must be some way to use all the information that I had learned about Drugor to my advantage. Point by point, I went over everything I knew about the Jhinn, his body, and his ship. After weighing all the data that I could recall, I came up with an idea.

I had a plan, but it depended on two things. First, I would need a weapon. Drugor had taken the carbine with him, and I was banking on him bringing it back with him on his return. Second, I would need to act immediately upon his return. Drugor would waste no time in switching minds to regain his own body. I hoped to force him to switch, but on my terms.

If my plan failed, one of two things would happen: either Drugor would kill me, or I would kill him and end up in this freakish body forever.

I fell asleep rehearsing the plan in my mind.

* * *

By converting the ship's clock to Earth time, I figured Drugor had been out for almost two days. From this point on, I must spend every hour in the compartment where Drugor would enter the ship.

I removed the coveralls, then removed the protective undersuit. Discarding the undersuit, I slipped back into the coveralls. I then set out for the entry bay.

I positioned myself so as to catch him the instant he came through the airlock. It happened so quickly that I was almost thrown off guard. No sooner had I positioned myself than the hatch hissed open and Drugor stepped in. I recovered quickly, but my spirits plummeted when I saw that he was not carrying the carbine.

My eyes dropped to the utility belt, and something caught my attention. The hunting knife was still there, the ivory handle protruding from behind the belt. I knew that the knife would not be as effective as the carbine, but I hoped it would serve as my weapon.

I needed to alter my plans slightly. I must work at closer range than I cared to and my timing must be perfect. One slip and I'd be dead.

It was now or never. I roared in my growling voice and charged, hurling my powerful seven-foot frame toward the small human body occupied by Drugor. Drugor's human eyes widened with fear, and his hand immediately dropped to the utility belt. Just before reaching Drugor, I threw my hands up in the air, exposing my belly.

Abruptly, I found myself in my own body, facing a roaring seven-foot giant charging toward me, its arms raised. My hand went for the hunting knife. Before the surprised Drugor could react, I brought the knife up and plunged it into the vulnerable navel area of the Jhinn. Blood gushed from the wound as Drugor vainly tried to stop the flow with his hands. He staggered back a few feet and fell. The Jhinn was dead.

Drugor had not yet transmitted a report giving Earth's location. As far as the High Command was concerned Drugor had probably met with an accident somewhere in the vastness of space, as often happened to Jhinn scouts.

I keyed the studs on the utility belt to restore power to the ship's controls and seated myself at the control panel. Where, I wondered, would be a good place to land this ship? For a moment I was in a whimsical mood and considered landing at places like the White House lawn or Cape Canaveral. But I thought better of it. I'd probably be detained and interrogated by federal authorities, followed by barrages of questions by news reporters. Being a private person, the thought didn't appeal to me.

I flew over Blackroot Forest and spotted my pickup. Drugor had left it in the same clearing where I'd parked it. After flying the ship to a nearby Air Force base, I circled the base flying low and slow enough to make sure that their radar picked me up.

I flew back to the pickup, landed in the clearing, and sped away from the scene.

* * *

The next day there were news reports of UFO sightings over Blackroot State Forest. The Air Force investigated and announced, as I expected they would, that the sightings were nothing more than weather balloons.

Of Celestial Tourists

The canvas of the night
Leaks the light
Of faraway stars.
The tent of the sky
Provides little protection
From the curious gaze
Of these other worlds
Causing our suspicion
Of celestial tourists.

But, we ask ourselves
Why do they visit only
In outlying places
Or greet humans
Of dubious mental stability,

Or is it actually true
That the contacts are fantasy,
Our wishful thinking
To belie the fact
That we recognize we
Are beneath their interest.

— K. S. Hardy

PENANCE

By Gary Every

The young girl's sobs and moans brought rescuers rushing towards her. The crime of lust had been finished rather quickly, men of the rogue knight's character are never known for their stamina. This particular act of rape was no exception.

"Unhand my daughter!" the innkeeper shouted.

The errant knight laughed, "Come forth old man, I am not afraid to face you in battle."

The knight had slain countless infidels on the battlefield, murdered a handful of Christian souls in various misadventures, and a few more drops of blood on his guilt-stained hands would not matter much.

The innkeeper rushed forward, reckless of the danger, desperate to rescue his daughter.

The girl tried to scream but the knight covered her mouth with his hand. She bit the knight, her teeth gnashing at his chain mail. The knight held his sword aloft and waited in the darkness.

But the innkeeper was not alone—the mountain village was filled with good citizens who rushed to the rescue. Farmers came with pitchforks, hunters carried bows, and coopers wielded hammers. Even the blacksmith and his brawny sons rushed forward to aid the young maiden. The knight looked up the dark alleyway and saw the torches of an approaching lynch mob.

"They will kill you when they catch you," the girl laughed.

The knight spit, his phlegm landing on her belly button where her dress had been torn into tatters.

"Pig!" the girl cried.

"Knave," shouted the innkeeper, "Harm a hair on her head and we will stretch you on the rack before we hang you."

The knight scowled at the girl, uttered a curse word, then reached out with his sword, stirring his spit. The blade sliced her belly button, causing a thin trickle of blood to stream across her stomach.

The girl cried out and the mob surged forward, close enough now for the blacksmith's sons to pelt the villain with cobblestones.

The knight turned and ran.

"May the devil keep your soul for all damnation," the innkeeper shouted, waving his fist.

* * *

Step after step the knight kept running and running, easily outdistancing the lynch mob. The knight continued running, step after step falling in the dark. He soon left the mountain village far behind, running through the forest, breathlessly scurrying through the mist and fog. And still he kept running, one foot after another.

The forest path began to close in, twigs and branches clutching at his clothing. The infernal fog disguised the rocks inside misty shrouds and the knight stumbled.

Splash.

The knight's misplaced step landed in a small pond. Startled, the knight stopped running and sat down on a log. He gulped down big swallows of air trying to catch his breath. His head swam with dizziness and he had to take a moment to remember why he had been running in the first place.

Then it all came flashing back to him: the beautiful young girl, the rape, and the lynch mob. The knight sighed; it was not the angry villagers who had forced him to run like a frightened deer.

It was the words of the innkeeper, a warning about hellfire and damnation. As he grew older the medieval knight found himself growing more and more afraid of the afterlife. For a man with as many crimes on his hands as the knight had on his there was only one eternal-resting place—Satan's home.

A small water snake began to swim across the pond, crossing the knight's reflection.

For a man such as himself the cost of penance would be high, perhaps impossible.

Suddenly the snake dipped beneath the water. The knight's reflection rippled beneath the swimming snake, the image blurred. As the waters stilled, the knight's face was replaced with a skull—flames draped over the ears like hair. The knight screamed and dropped his sword, the blade sinking into the ooze at the bottom of the pond.

* * *

The knight stood and stared at the flaming skull for the longest time. It was the knight's torso, his cloak and shirt, arms and legs, but there was a flaming skull atop the shoulders where his head belonged. As long as the knight did not move the reflection did not move.

Stalemate.

The knight scanned the dark and murky waters for any trace of his fallen weapon. Every time he shifted there was the burning skull gazing at him with red, hot coal eyes.

"Be gone demon." The knight held up his fingers in the sign of the cross.

"A sinner such as you dares to invoke the sign of the cross," the demon laughed.

"What is it you want!" the knight cried out.

"I heard you are seeking penance." The burning skull hissed. "There is an eccentric monk on the far side of the bridge who has a reputation for giving easy penance to wealthy men. They say the richer the man the easier the penance."

The knight smiled, "Where is this eccentric monk?"

"Are you a rich man?" the skull hissed.

"Anywhere there is a road with wealthy travelers and a few choice ambush sites I am a rich man," the knight said.

The burning skull laughed.

* * *

Rattle.

Rattle.

Roll.

The knight marched further and further into the forest, following the directions of the burning skull to the eccentric monk and the easy penance.

Rattle, rattle, roll. The sounds echoed through the forest. The knight marched onwards, cutting through the fog, following a faint path that wound past thorn, briar, and bramble, but that sound stayed in front of him as he moved, always just ahead.

The knight came to a bridge and hurried across. It was one of those bridges which people always hurry over. The knight stumbled and there was a grunt and grumble from under the bridge, like something awakening from a snoring slumber. The knight hustled away.

Rattle, rattle, roll.

From amidst a thicket, the knight fought thorn and root to wrestle his way into a clearing. There was nothing in the clearing except a well and barrel.

There was silence.

The knight turned to leave.

Rattle, rattle, roll.

He spun back around and now beside the barrel and well was a small stone building. Looking in the window the knight could see a monk's cowl with a right arm flailing again and again.

Rattle, rattle, roll.

The knight crept up to the window and discovered the monk playing dice The white cubes rattled in the cup before the monk sent them tumbling and rolling across the table.

Rattle, rattle, roll.

"Snake eyes!" the monk exulted. "You there, at the window!" the monk shouted, without removing his hood. "Why do you bother me—I am busy now."

"I have come seeking penance for my sins."

"There are probably a lot of them, too." The monk sighed, "And many heinous crimes on your hands, too."

The knight nodded.

"Are you a rich man?"

The knight held up a sack of gold.

"There is a barrel beside the well," the monk tossed the dice again, "Fill the barrel up with water and you are forgiven."

* * *

The knight walked over to the well, picked up the barrel, and dunked it. The barrel looked unremarkable but when the knight pulled it up from the icy water not a single drop had gotten inside. The knight dunked the barrel into the well again and again but the inside of the barrel never got wet. The barrel looked unremarkable in every way but it was obviously enchanted.

With a curse word the knight abandoned the thought of

penance, tossed the barrel on to the ground and stormed off into the forest. The knight tried to retrace his path but the trail was more difficult to follow from the other direction. There were rustling noises in the forest, something scurrying through the underbrush. The gnarled trees clutched at his clothing, the brambles tore his flesh, and the twigs scratched and jabbed at his face.

Splat.

The knight fell face first on to the forest floor. He found himself face to face with a pair of red glowing eyes, watching him from a thicket. The eyes disappeared into the dark shadows, moving swiftly.

The knight returned to his feet and ran, crashing through the underbrush. The red eyes followed, they would appear and disappear at different places on the trail, the left, the right— appearing, disappearing. Frightened, the knight put his head down and charged, sprinting along the forest path. The knight howled like a banshee as he ran, hoping to frighten whatever manner of forest beast was chasing him.

When he was too breathless to howl any longer the knight kept running some more. The red eyes kept pace, panting in the darkness. Then the knight noticed one pair of red eyes on the left and another pair on the right. The beasts themselves began to howl. As the knight ran they nipped at his heels. The knight could hear other members of the pack join in the hunt.

The knight realized now what lived beneath the bridge—a pack of wolves, a coven of hellhounds. The knight suddenly came up to the bridge where the leader of the pack stood sentry, snarling and foaming. The three-headed dog howled, each mouth glistening with rows of fangs, challenging the knight.

Reluctantly, the knight turned around to conclude his unfinished business with the eccentric monk.

* * *

The knight returned to the clearing with the well but the stone building had disappeared. The knight walked over and retrieved the discarded barrel. He went to leave.

Rattle, rattle, roll.

The knight noticed something unusual about the surface of the well water. Reflected on top of the water a pair of dice made from bones rolled and tumbled, numbers painted on all six sides. The dice both came up ones.

"Snake eyes," the monk shouted. His reflection replaced that of the dice.

"Why have you given me this enchanted barrel?" the knight cried out.

"Because I love to assign penance to rich men," the monk laughed, "But rarely do rich men enjoy the penance that I assign them."

The monk pulled back his hood and revealed his face for the first time. It was the wicked grin of the burning skull.

* * *

The wolves slept soundly beneath the bridge and let the knight pass without incident. At the far side of the bridge the knight knelt upon the bank and dipped the barrel in the river. It remained empty.

The knight followed the river on its journey to the sea. He dunked the barrel beneath waterfalls but it did not fill. At roaring rapids where giant white water rivers came together the barrel remained dry even when the knight got soaking wet and nearly drowned. At marsh, lagoon, pond, and granite pool the barrel did not fill. The knight followed the river all the way to the ocean, striding off the edge of the pier and falling into the harbor with a splash. The knight sputtered for breath in the ocean, clinging to the floating barrel, but the inside of the barrel remained dry.

He tried to fill the barrel at desert oasis and mountain springs. He tried healing waters and twice-blessed sprinkles. Once the knight caught the first snowflake of winter but even this magic charm did not fill the barrel. The knight wandered the earth for years and years, decades and decades, seeking penance.

* * *

The reflection of the wrinkled, white-haired old man made the knight drop his barrel in disbelief The knight had traveled deserts and oceans, valleys and caves, during his quest and now it was the reflection of an old man that stopped him.

The knight had climbed a high rugged peak to reach a tiny mountain spring whose bubbling waters were legendary for their purity. The knight knelt beside the pool and readied to dip the barrel one more time when he was frightened by the reflection of a white-haired old man.

It was the knight's own reflection.

All those years searching for penance had taken their toll. His handsome good looks were now weathered and wrinkled. His muscles had melted into gray hair. The knight had spent years carrying a magic barrel that never filled with water. He was no longer the powerful warrior who had committed many crimes long ago but was now a frail and lonely old man. He had wasted his youth. The knight sighed and put the barrel down, leaving it beside the spring as he walked to the nearest village.

* * *

The dinner inside his belly felt good. There was a tankard of ale next to his chair and the knight propped his feet up beside the fire. It felt good to relax, not worry about weighty matters such as penance and eternal damnation.

"Missing your sweetheart?" the innkeeper asked, her foul breath pushing over her lips like a blast of arctic chill.

The knight's arm was crooked over the chair as if he was still carrying the barrel.

"No," the knight took a sip from his ale. "I always travel alone."

The knight straightened out his arm, stretched, and laughed. He undid his shoes, making himself comfortable, wiggling his toes in front of the fire.

The innkeeper began to massage his feet. She goosed him.

"If you are traveling alone then perhaps you are interested in some of the other services our tavern has to offer," she winked lewdly.

The knight snarfled in surprise, "Old woman you are as fat and bloated as a dung beetle."

"I bet it has been a long time since you received any loving, hasn't it old timer?" the innkeeper teased him.

It had been years and years. The last time the knight had experienced any carnal delights had been the night of the terrible crime that had ruined his life. That was rape and hardly love. The knight was not sure that he had ever felt love.

"You've got webbed toes," the innkeeper said, "That is a sign of royalty. My son," she continued, "has got webbed toes."

The innkeeper called to her son and he dutifully lumbered over beside the fire. He was a little old to still be called a boy, clumsy and ugly, drooling—probably the village idiot, the knight mused. The lad began to remove his shoes to show off his webbed toes and immediately an overwhelming stench began to fill the room.

"Wench," the knight cried out, "I am weary from my journeys, bring me another tankard of ale and leave me alone."

The innkeeper had her son fetch another tankard of ale and left the knight alone as he requested. The knight sipped at his ale and fell asleep in front of the fireplace. Perhaps it was because of the flames so near to his closed eyelids but the knight dreamt of fire and brimstone all evening long.

* * *

Sweat covered his brow when he awoke suddenly, just before the dawn. He was frightened at the prospect of spending all eternity condemned to damnation. The knight rose from the chair and began to march towards the mountain spring to retrieve the barrel.

The knight hastily scrambled up the mountain path, kicking stones as he hurried. What if someone else had found the barrel and taken it home during the night? The knight raced to the mountain pool, eager to be the first one to arrive at the break of day.

The knight reached the pool and the barrel was still exactly where he had left it. He rushed to the shore, dropped to his knees, and dipped the barrel into the crystal clear mountain waters.

Dry.

A voice cackled with laughter. The knight was not alone.

"Why you old pervert," the innkeeper chuckled, "Coming up here to spy on me while I bathe. You Peeping Tom."

"I assure you madam," the knight replied indignantly. "That if I were such a rogue as to be a Peeping Tom, I would pick a much younger, prettier, lady. No offense intended."

"You don't like what you see," the innkeeper laughed as she displayed her birthday suit.

The knight's jaw dropped in amazement. This woman had a scar on her belly button—a scar from a sword.

"I used to be young and beautiful once," the innkeeper sighed, "But I lost my virginity when I was raped. I was impregnated by the villain and gave birth to my only son. After that, no decent man would marry me. When my father died I inherited the inn but few travelers come through this high mountain pass anymore. I was forced to become a whore to feed my son."

The knight was stunned. He had spent all these years seeking forgiveness for his crime without ever once considering the victim. That the knight had ruined his life because of his own crime seemed fair but to have ruined the life of another, through no fault of her own, hardly seemed fair. He had never considered how his crime had changed the life of his victim. She too had been denied love.

The knight's lower lip trembled; his eyes welled up with water. He wanted to apologize. He was ashamed to admit he was a criminal to a woman who did not recognize him. Besides, words alone would never repair the harm he done so long ago.

The thought of the harm he had caused the woman made the knight cry and that first tear filled the barrel.

* * *

At the moment when the first tear filled the barrel the knight's face underwent a startling magical transformation. As the first tear washed away years of misery, guilt, and sin, the innkeeper's daughter thought she had never seen a man so handsome and noble. The knight looked up to see the woman staring at him with admiring eyes. Ashamed, he turned his gaze downwards, staring into the barrel. He was stunned to realize that the barrel was full.

The astonished knight stared at the woman's reflection atop the surface of the water inside the barrel. It was not the reflection of the aged and wrinkled innkeeper but the reflection of the young and nubile woman she once been, many years ago.

The knight looked up to see the old woman still smiling at him. He realized that the beautiful young woman she had once been, still lived inside that smile.

"Forgive me," he croaked hoarsely.

"Forgive you for what?" she asked.

The knight could not bear to confess his crime from long ago.

"Forgive me," the knight pleaded, "For not having gold, jewels, or roses to offer as a gift but only this beat-up old barrel."

"It is a rather ordinary looking barrel too," she said, "At least you can carry it back to the inn for me so I can offer my customers fresh water."

The knight carried the barrel full of water back to the inn. Then he chopped some firewood, did the dishes, and swept the kitchen. The knight decided he liked living at the inn; especially the way the innkeeper smiled at him. He hunted venison for the table, fixed the roof, and started a garden. And every morning, just before sunrise, the knight took the barrel up to the mountain spring and returned with it full of water.

One night, most unexpectedly, the innkeeper gave her carnal love to the knight willingly. The knight was flabbergasted. He had never suspected what a powerful aphrodisiac true love could be.

The knight discovered another unexpected treasure. Every time he gazed at his true love's reflection in water, her image was once again young and beautiful. The knight and the innkeeper married and the town's people commented what a happy couple they seemed, and especially the village gossips noted their eccentric habit of bathing together so frequently.

The Gnostic

Cuffed to my flesh I felt like a prisoner,
My soul sewn to sinew and chained to bone.
To escape this feral resolve of matter
As sensitive to Spirit as stone,
I studied the mystics with great fervor.
I sat at my small desk each night alone,
Believing I could burst into the Unknown.
If I should break through a saint's line of words—
Literally squeeze through them to the other side—
I'd know the freedom gained by soaring birds.
Then one night while reading I felt myself slide
Right through the O in oneness to where
As vacuous nonessence of no-air,
I wish again I had a body to wear.

— Kenneth O'Keefe

ANGELS

By David B. Riley

I'd just established a fire and was letting out my new bedroll so it could collect dust, when Paul suddenly took off down the trail. A few minutes later, he was back, nuzzling a jet-black mare that looked a lot like he did. I was more curious about the woman riding her. She was gorgeous, a complete knockout. She climbed off her horse and straightened out a rather frilly French-cut blue dress. This brunette with eyes like shining emeralds smiled at me. She had the prettiest smile. "You must be Miles," she said.

I had to think for a second, and then I remembered that was my name. "Yes ma'am."

She looked at the fire. "Do you have any more coffee?"

That was a funny thing. I don't recall making any. But there was my little blue pot sitting on some coals. I knocked the dust from my spare cup and poured some. She graciously accepted and took a sip. "This is terrible coffee."

"I know. It's all I got."

She invited herself to sit down on the log I was sitting on. "Miles, my name's Janus. I'm not from around here."

"Neither am I," I pointed out.

"I'm an angel, Miles," she explained.

"I never met an angel before," I said, having my usual penchant for stating the obvious. "At least, not as I recall."

"Well, we don't get out much." She took another sip, then poured the rest out on the ground. "Horrible."

"You're sure pretty enough to be an angel." And that was the truth.

"Miles," she hesitated for just a moment, "I'm from hell. Most mortals don't realize there are angels in hell."

"I did not know that."

"Back during the troubles, some of us left heaven. Anyway, I'm an angel from hell. Do you have a problem with that?"

"Heck no. Nick, he seemed to treat me fair enough. I give pert near everyone a chance."

She smiled. "That's sweet, Miles."

"Why does an angel from hell come all the way out here? Don't get me wrong, I'm glad you stopped by," I said. "Just a might bit curious."

"I understand." She put her hand on my knee. "Nick wanted you to have a little reward."

"What kind of reward?" I asked. I'd gotten his chest back for him, but hadn't seen him in the month that had gone by since then.

She laughed. "Me, silly." She stood up and snapped her fingers. The pretty blue dress vanished in a shower of golden sparks. She was not wearing any undergarments. "You can have me if you fancy me. Mind you, once you've had me, no mortal woman will ever satisfy you again."

Fancy her? I can't fully describe how beautiful she was. That guy who made the statue of Venus could've easily used her for a model. She kissed me and knocked me down onto the bedroll. "Miles, I know you live in a sexually repressed time. Oh, I miss the Romans." She started undoing my trousers. "Just relax. You might enjoy this."

Well, "enjoy" was an understatement. I still don't know what they call what she did to me. But I sure did enjoy it. I must've dozed off. When I woke, it was daylight. She was still lying next to me, stark naked. She was awake and seemed to have been watching me.

"You're sweet, Miles. I've gotta go now." She stood up and whistled. That mare came trotting up fast. She climbed on its back, still naked as a jaybird. "I'm going to flash some miners down the road, then head home." She hesitated a second, then the horse ran off and she was gone.

I noticed Paul was also gazing off longingly. "Hey Paul, time to get going."

* * *

I'd decided to return to California and see if I could get fired at something other than mining for a while. It was almost like coming home. Stockton was where I first got fired. I checked Paul into a livery and then was looking for a place for me, when I noticed the Oriental Bath House and Massage Parlor. I decided I'd spend some of my remaining money and went right in. A matronly woman looked me over. She was no more oriental than I was. Then I noticed a bevy of Chinese girls giggling off in a nearby hallway. I was instructed to go to room three and get undressed. I did as I was told, after parting with a whole quarter.

Two Chinese women poured hot water down my back. After three such dousings, they left me to soak by myself. I was debating whether to pay more and get a massage when the door opened and a woman entered. She was behind me, so it wasn't until she moved around to my front that I could see her. I tried to cover my privates as best I could.

"So you're Miles," she said.

"That's what they call me," I said. "You have the advantage."

She was stunning, every bit as pretty as Janus, but with soft blonde hair and eyes that were bluer than blue, like little pieces of a cobalt jar. "Miles, I guess you already suspect, I'm an angel."

"They say you can only see an angel if it wants you to," I said.

"And, once you've seen us, we can't conceal ourselves from you," she added. She pulled up a chair. "My name's Buffy."

"What kind of name is that?" I asked, then regretted it.

"A very old one," she said with a cross tone.

"Miles, when someone like Nick takes a personal interest in a mortal, we do get a bit concerned," Buffy explained. "That's why I'm here."

"Who's we?" I asked, as a certain unease filled my innards.

"Miles, I'm from heaven. I'm concerned about you, Miles. That bunch from hell, they're not to be trusted, or taken lightly."

"Well, I don't trust 'em, exactly. I don't know what to make of things. I'm just a simple clod from Kansas," I argued.

"A simple clod who has a first name relationship with Nick Mephistopheles. And I don't even want to think what sort of depravity Janus is leading you into." She started for the door. "I'll see you, Miles."

I finished my bath and got dressed. I found my horse being petted by a very pretty redheaded woman dressed in one of those

Parisian dresses, this one was green and black. She had the prettiest eyes I'd ever seen, even prettier than Buffy or Janus. She smiled.

"His name's Paul," I said.

She patted him again. "I know that."

I was really wondering why I was so popular with the angels all of a sudden. "I'm Miles."

"I know that." She finally turned toward me. "What did Buffy want?"

"Who are you?" I inquired.

"Oh, I'm sorry. It's just that I feel I already know you. I've heard so much about you," she explained. She extended a dainty hand. She was a little smaller than Janus, but reminded me of her with the same sassy look. "I'm an angel, Miles. And I'm not from heaven."

I gladly took her hand. "How many angels are there in hell?"

"Just a few of us. And those silly demons are so jealous." She seemed to regret that admission. "Is Buffy trying to woo you back to their side?"

"I ain't on anyone's side," I pointed out.

"Did she give you a peck on the cheek, or just a crummy handshake?" she asked.

"I still don't know your name," I said, trying to change the subject.

"Mabel." She was not going to give up easily. "Well?"

"Neither. She never touched me."

Mabel smiled. "God has forbidden angels from touching mortals." She shrugged, then she suddenly grabbed me and kissed me. "Of course, I don't really care what God wants. I haven't worked for Him in ages."

I can't fully describe why kissing her was so much nicer than kissing a regular woman. And I hadn't kissed all that many regular women. But it was. And I was having trouble keeping my wits about me.

"You want to go back into the bath house and take a bath with me?" Mabel asked.

"No," I said.

She seemed surprised. "Buffy must've really impressed you."

I shook my head. "I want to go check into a hotel room with you."

She smiled. "Oh, Miles."

Mabel turned out to be every bit as satisfying as Janus. I didn't know why I rated so much attention, but was sure enjoying myself. The next morning she was still with me, lying on top of me with her head on my shoulder. "Miles, maybe we can do a threesome some time."

"Threesome?"

"You should read some of those French novels, Miles." She got up and started getting dressed. Her clothes had not vanished in a display of sparks. "You, me, and Janus next time."

That sounded like something beyond my simple imagination. But it didn't sound unpleasant. "Okay."

As she arranged herself while looking in the mirror, she said, "Buffy is God's personal secretary. You sure got their attention, Miles."

"Personal secretary? "

"Yes Miles. Am I as pretty as Buffy?" she asked.

"And then some." I wasn't really sure about that, but I wasn't stupid enough to tell her anything else. She beamed as she admired herself in the mirror.

"Who's Nick's personal secretary?" I reasoned that if God had one, so would Nick.

"Janus, silly." She offered no explanation about her own role in the hierarchy of angels. When she'd gotten the look she wanted, she opened the door and left without any further formalities.

I got hired right away in Stockton, at the Palace Barber Shop cutting hair. I'd never actually done humans before, but the dogs I'd trimmed always seemed happy enough. Folks would come from miles away with their longhaired dogs when I was growing up. After three hours, no one complained and I'd even gotten a few tips. Then some boat captain wanted a shave.

It's amazing how much the human face can bleed before it stops. They didn't even fire me. I was expected back the next day, so I headed off to Mrs. Bunyan's rooming house. I arrived just in time for supper. We had ham with mashed potatoes and some sort of greens. It was right tasty and included with the rent. As I relaxed with the other borders, two old women who smelled funny and some guy just out of the cavalry, Mrs. Bunyan approached me with an odd expression on her face. "Mister O'Malley."

I looked at her, expecting more words. "Yes?" I finally asked.

"There's a gentleman to see you. He's in the back yard. Refuses to come inside."

I picked myself up from the too-low chair and followed her to the back door. I looked out. It was very dark. And there was somebody there, somebody very large standing in the yard, wearing a top hat. As I approached, I recognized him. Ellul looked completely out of place wearing a jacket and top hat. In the darkness, he could nearly pass for a large man. "Ellul?"

"Mister wants to see you."

I shrugged. "Sure. Where is he?"

"In his office," the demon in the top hat explained.

"Uh, where might that be?" I already was afraid I knew the answer.

"In his office. We go now." He had a white horse. He climbed up on it. He seemed to expect me to do the same.

I hesitated. "I'll get my horse."

I jogged three blocks to the livery. Paul was in the wrong stall, a stall with an Appaloosa mare. I tossed his saddle on his back. When I had him saddled up, he stood there and didn't move. "Dang it, Paul. You are my horse, and for once, let's do what I want." The horse reluctantly started moving. He didn't seem at all pleased to see Ellul.

We rode along in silence for the better part of an hour, and then we turned onto a narrow trail that turned onto a still narrower one. It reminded me more of a deer trail than a path for horse traffic. We entered a dark railway tunnel. "How'd they get into hell before the railroads?" That remark went unanswered. Our tunnel branched off into another one. Then, finally, we stopped at a gate. And I do mean stopped. Paul planted his hooves and would not budge. I climbed down.

"We go on foot. Not much farther," Ellul announced.

This gate was rusted over and kind of tilted. Ellul opened it and I followed him inside. Then he shut it. There didn't seem to be any lock on it.

Ellul seemed to know my thoughts. "Mortals and spirits cannot pass, unless it is opened." We walked a few paces, then he added, "Only demons can open the gates of hell."

That meant, if interpreted literally, I'd just willingly walked into hell and could never return unless they allowed me to. So, I put my hands in my pockets and strolled along with a demon. The first thing that hit me was the place is uncomfortably warm. And it stinks. The source of the aroma soon became apparent. We rounded a bend and there was the famous fiery lake. It was bigger than I'd expected. The odor of brimstone wafted off the water and permeated the surrounding air. It was actually kind of pretty, with the yellow flames reflecting off the turquoise water. Some sort of algae seemed to give the water its color.

Ellul blurted out "It stinks," as we walked along, "like sewer." We soon arrived at a row of chariots. He climbed aboard one and I followed. Then a team of young naked men raced up and into the harnesses. And we started moving. We entered a city that overlooked the lake. I was being looked over by a lot of different folks. I guess demons didn't drive ordinary people around in chariots very often.

I suppose the people were, or had been, dead. How this all works was never really explained to me. But they were there, looking out windows of their tall apartment house buildings. As we moved further into town, the buildings seemed to get bigger. And, in the center, was an ornate, maybe even gaudy, palace perched on a slight hill, making it just barely the tallest structure around. It reminded me of Egyptian styling, though I'd only seen a few pictures of buildings in Egypt, so I wasn't sure.

Ellul once again seemed to anticipate what I was thinking. "Based on the Library at Alexandria, before it was burned. Crummy copy." Something brown and smelly landed on top one of the chariot pullers. Ellul immediately hurled a fireball off in the direction it had originated from. I never did see the actual attacker. "We're here." The chariot stopped. "Go up the steps."

I did. The chariot and Ellul drove away. As I went inside, I was confronted by a really big demon. "Who are you supposed to be?"

"Miles O'Malley. I'm expected."

"I'm not expecting you," he countered.

"I am here to see Mister Mephistopheles."

He let out a laugh. "Now I know you're lying. Nobody ever wants to see him. What are you going to steal?"

I didn't really care for his attitude. "I am here to see Mister Mephistopheles. I will be sure to let him know who kept me waiting."

He shrugged. "Go on then." He pointed down a long marble corridor. "Down the hall, through the big doors."

So, I ventured down the hall and through the big doors. And, on the other side of the doors sat ten demons, all in a row. Next to them was a regular sized door. The one nearest the door stood and opened the door. "Mister O'Malley to see his greatness."

Inside that door sat Janus, behind a really immense wooden desk. She came around and hugged me. She was wearing about the flimsiest thing I'd ever seen. It didn't conceal much. It was a short white dress, loose at the top and barely covering her lower intimacies. She obviously was not wearing undergarments. "Miles." She pointed at a chair. "Sit down, Miles." I did. To my surprise, she sat on my lap and put her head on my shoulder. "My hair doesn't smell like shit." She was right about that.

"Mabel says you want to do a threesome." She started licking my ear. "I can't wait." Then she looked toward a door on the side of the office. "Oh pooh." She got off of me. "He'll see you now." She ventured over to the door and opened it.

This office was very nicely furnished. It had a sort of earthy color scheme. I recognized a few Navajo patterns on rugs hanging on the walls. A barrel cactus was growing in a pot in the corner. One wall was mostly a huge picture window, providing a view of the fiery lake. Janus seated me, then left.

A moment later, another door opened and Nick entered. "Miles." I shook his clammy hand. "Miles, good to see you again." He was holding a violin, which he placed against the wall. "Fellow bet me he could outplay me. Wagered his soul against a few more years as president of his country. I play a mean fiddle, Miles." He sat down at his modest desk that was half the size of Janus's. "He gave up in thirty seconds." Nick opened up a wooden box. "Packed it right in. Cigar, Miles?"

"No thanks. I don't smoke," I replied.

"You should. You'll live longer. Reduces stress," Nick explained. He lit up his cigar. "Ah."

"Quite a place you've got here."

"Isn't it?" He took another long drag on his cigar. "Miles, seems we've got a bit of a problem." He opened his desk drawer and removed a drawing. "This is the angel, Ralph."

It, like Buffy, seemed an odd name for an angel. "Ralph?"

"Yes, Ralph. It seems he's gone up to earth for some reason. At first, I just thought he'd made peace with God and run back to heaven. Well, that was rather silly on my part. Now, he's supposedly in the Sacramento River area working in the maritime industry."

"On a barge?"

"Or perhaps a ferry or something. We can't have this Miles. We simply can't. It's one thing to go out for a message, but angels can't live with the mortals. It just isn't the way things are done." Nick snuffed out his cigar into a black obsidian ashtray. "Miles, I need you to take Ellul and go and fetch him back."

"What if he won't come?" I asked.

"Then you'll have to kill him," Nick coldly stated. "Now, I know that sounds cruel. It's not like he was ever alive, in a mortal sense, anyway."

I didn't really understand what he meant. "I don't want to do this."

Undaunted, he placed a box of bullets on the desk. "There's a metal called titanium. It's not used much. It requires high temperatures to work it. And it's too hard for bullets. That's why these are titanium, with a silver coating. Consider them very expensive."

"I don't want to do this."

He continued unfazed, "Now, an angel has limited power on Earth. But, be careful. He can easily confuse or trick you. If he won't come back with Ellul, shoot him. This titanium, most mortals have no idea it's what the Greek Olympian gods used to kill off the Titans. They made spears out of it. That's why the metal is named after them. It can kill an angel. And I'd just as soon that not be widely known." He stood up and picked up his fiddle.

"I've got an engagement. I'm playing down by the lake. I'm really good, Miles. Pity, you won't have time to hear me," Nick boasted.

"I don't want to do this," I told an empty room.

The door behind me opened. "Ellul is here for you," Janus said.

"I don't want to do this," I repeated as I followed her down the long corridor to the front of the building.

"I thought there was only one God. What's all this talk about the Olympians and Titans?"

She shrugged. "Sure, there's one now." She stuck out her chest, just a bit, to change the subject and divert my attention from thinking. "Mortal women were designed after angels like me and Mabel, Miles," Janus said. Then she grabbed me and kissed me. "See you." Then she waved at Ellul, snapped her fingers, and disappeared with a shower of sparks.

It took me a moment to recover from her kiss. I staggered down the marble steps and climbed aboard the chariot. We had only gone one block when a glob of brown stuff landed on the head of the boy right in front of me, the last in the line of pullers. Ellul reared back his powerful arm and hurled a fireball. I had not previously been all that impressed with these fireballs. But this one struck some bloke square in the chest, knocking him down. The flames engulfed him and he ran away screaming."

Unconcerned with the recent event, Ellul asked "You like angel? You like Janus?"

"Yes, I like her." How could I not like her? My knees were still weak, just from her kiss.

"She has the job that should go to a demon," he said. I couldn't tell if he was jealous or simply filling me in.

"I'm told the angel Buffy has a similar job in heaven." I didn't want to upset him, but I saw a real opportunity to get some answers here about things mortals, like me, just guess at.

"Buffy has the job of a cherub," Ellul said. "We don't have archangels in hell, but she's even over them. She is only an angel. When Mister found out God made Buffy his secretary, Janus was suddenly his secretary. He never even had a secretary before then. No one ever wants to see him."

"Oh." I was completely at a loss for words. "God sent his own secretary to see me on Earth?"

"No. She was sent to find the angel Ralph," Ellul said.

That deflated my head a little bit. "Oh."

"Buffy very pretty," he said as he yanked the reins and the boys pulling us increased their pace. He was right about that, too.

Paul and Ellul's horse were waiting right where we'd left them. We were soon out of the railroad tunnel and on our way back to Stockton. I had to barber the next day, so I caught up with Ellul at his campsite that evening. "So, how do we find him?" I asked.

He pointed out at the water. "There's the river. We wait until he comes by," Ellul said.

"That's it? What if he doesn't come by? We've got a drawing of him," I argued. "We can ask questions."

"I don't look like you," Ellul replied. "I scare people. People are afraid of demons."

He had a point. The only reason I hadn't run away from him when I first saw him was on account of my foot being stuck under an ore track. "Well, how 'bout I ask around and you can wait here and keep an eye on the river?"

"Okay."

Paul and I headed for town. Then he stopped so fast he nearly threw me. Buffy was standing next to the riverbank, gazing out at the water.

"Hello Miles. I was just looking for an old friend. I thought he might be on that ferry out there. He isn't."

"You mean Ralph?" I asked.

"You know about him?" She seemed somewhat alarmed.

"Sure, Ellul's down the river doing the same thing." I wondered if that was a wise admission. "I was going into town, to ask around."

"How did you get involved in this?" she cautiously asked me.

"Nick asked me to help find him."

"Can I ride with you?"

"Sure."

She climbed up behind me and put her arms around my waist. Her hair did not smell like shit, either. "Miles, you have an advantage in finding Ralph. Angels can sense when another one is around."

"And I'm not an angel," I said, always stating the obvious. "But I can see them."

"Exactly." She kind of gave me a little squeeze. Then she eased up and tapped my sidearm. "Uh, what kind of bullets are you carrying in there?"

"These ones Nick gave me," I replied. "Titan something."

"Titanium?"

"That's it."

"Nick gave you titanium bullets?" Her voice seemed higher. "You realize, that Nick himself is vulnerable to them? And he just gave them to you?" she asked.

I had not really thought of that. "Yep, just handed them over." I could kill the devil. It was an intriguing idea. But Nick had been good to me.

"Miles, no matter what happens, you must destroy those bullets when this is over. No matter what. Promise me," she demanded.

"You don't want me to shoot Nick?"

"No. Absolutely not. Hell is a terrible place and Nick is an unbelievable jerk. But, can you imagine what it would be like if he weren't there to keep order? Until God says to kill him, and only then, don't even think about it. Understand?"

"Okay," I agreed.

She gave me another squeeze. "I sure hope we don't have to kill him. Nick must think we will."

"Where do we look?" I asked.

"The wharf area. I hope he's not upstairs with a saloon girl."

"Why's that?" I asked reflexively, without thinking.

"Angels, copulating with mortals, it makes me sick just thinking about it." After a few seconds went by, she added "Oh no. Miles, well, I still feel that way."

I pulled back on Paul's reins. "He's here."

"What?" Buffy asked. She seemed startled. "You're sure?" She looked around. "How do you know?"

"He's sitting on the porch reading the newspaper." I pointed at the boarding house across the street. It was too expensive, or I'd be living there.

"Oh." Buffy slid down. I followed her.

"Ain't going back," the angel Ralph declared. He looked at Buffy. "Been a long time."

"I don't have much reason to go to hell, Ralph," Buffy replied. She looked over at me. "This is Miles."

"I know who he is," Ralph said. "Nick's little errand boy."

"Nick's little errand boy was sent here to kill you," Buffy pointed out. "You can't just live here. It's not right."

"I work on a barge. Who am I hurting?" Ralph asked. "I keep a real plain and simple life."

"Mortals. This is their world, not yours," Buffy said. "It's just not allowed. And you know it."

Ralph neatly folded up his newspaper and placed it on the spotless wooden porch. Then he stood up. "I ain't going back, Buffy. Hell, it didn't turn out like we'd hoped. Nick, he's just another egomaniac trying to outdo God."

"You can either go back to hell, or you can come up to heaven and plead your case with God. That's it. You have no other choices," Buffy said.

"Odd, Nick and God being on the same side," Ralph said.

"Odd or not, which is it going to be?" she asked.

"Neither." And he was off. Boy could he run fast.

He was at least a hundred yards down the road before I could get back in the saddle. I was confident—no matter how fast this renegade angel could trot along, Paul could go faster. We were soon bearing down on him. Then, he jumped right into the Sacramento River and started swimming. In spite of my commands and pleas, Paul showed no willingness to go into the water to pursue him.

I ran along on foot for a ways, then jumped into a boat. I was able to row fast enough to keep him from gaining on me, yet I could not generate enough speed to overtake him. I did not really know how long this would go on, as I was not chasing any ordinary man. So, for the better part of an hour, I rowed and he swam. Then, I heard a yelp out of him and he disappeared below the waves in a flurry of bubbles. By the time I arrived upon his last location, all was quiet and there was no sign of him anyplace. I sat there in the river for a few minutes, and then I realized this point was familiar. It was where Ellul had camped out. Sure enough, a bunch of foamy bubbles soon appeared near the bank and Ellul and Ralph emerged from the water. Ellul had him by his privates. He threw the angel down hard on the bank. I rowed over and beached the boat. Buffy soon arrived on Paul.

"What do we do with him now?" I asked.

"Give me the gun," Ellul demanded.

"Don't do it, Miles," Buffy warned. "Remember what I said."

The angel Ralph looked at me. "Well, you gonna shoot me or what?"

"You willing to go back to hell?" I asked.

"No."

I drew the revolver out of the holster. "Then I guess I'll have to."

"Miles, don't," Buffy warned.

"He won't go back to hell." I cocked the hammer back. "Sorry pal."

Then there was a flurry of air all around us, and everything bristled with static electricity. Then, in a flash, both Buffy and Ralph were gone. I holstered the weapon.

"What happened to him?" Ellul asked. He usually knew more than I did.

I'd sensed all along that Buffy wanted to bring him back to heaven, even though Ralph wasn't particularly welcome there. "I think Buffy took him back to heaven."

"Mister won't like it," Ellul said.

I shrugged my shoulders. "Tell him to take it up with God. Ain't nothing we can do about it."

Ellul climbed up on his horse. "I go scare some children, then go back to hell."

"Sounds like a plan," I agreed.

Supernatural Love

In the tameless craving of the soundless night,
When sleep nor dream nor human love will due,
As the silver sliver of pale moonlight
Writhes through the twisted blind, I think of you.
No, not of you alone but of us both
Entwined in the frothing fire of love,
Merged in its ordeal of desire, where our growth
To oneness cancels all else I once dreamt of.

Yours are the arms that singe my pale flesh,
Yours the tongue that burns the knot of my heart,
And the mouth that melts my bones to lava red.

Angel or succubus from some hellish
Depth is matterless. For just to be apart
From you makes intolerable hell of my bed.

— Kenneth O'Keefe

FOR APPEARANCES' SAKE

By Justin R. Lawfer

"Cursed mountain," I muttered as I pulled myself onto a wide rocky ledge. I crawled toward the steep side of the mountain, then stopped to catch my breath. I looked up, mentally calculating how far I still had to climb.

"Why do wizards have to live in the most God-awful places?" I asked the rocky landform. I took a drink of lukewarm water from my flask, then stood up. I had been climbing since sunrise, and my entire body ached. My tunic was saturated with sweat. I hoped I was climbing the right side of the correct mountain, but so far I had not found the entrance to the wizard's home. This was leading me to the conclusion that no wizard lived in this mountain at all, and that the reports of his existence were nothing more than fables.

Suddenly, a man-shaped figure of shimmering blue light emerged from the rock wall before me. It waved its thin arms about in a menacing matter. I drew my sword. "Stay back!" I warned. The thing chuckled and continued to advance. I lashed out at its chest. The thing laughed again and then vanished. Behind it appeared the dark gaping entrance of a small cave.

"Enter!" a deep male voice commanded.

I walked into the cave, my hand firmly gripping the hilt of my sword. The cave walls were adorned with flaming torches, and the air was warm and moist. I stepped into a small chamber whose walls were lined with half a dozen torches, as well as dozens of long shelves. The shelves on the left side of the cave held jars and vials of strange liquids, while dozens of large books sat on the shelves on the right side of the cave.

A small man sat at a short table in the center of the cave. His head was covered with gray matted hair. A long, gray beard stretched from his chin and coiled like a snake onto the tabletop. He looked at me with cold blue eyes.

"Welcome," he said. Then he smiled.

A wave of disgust passed through me, for the wizard's teeth were a ghastly mess of black and crooked bones. I sheathed my sword and knelt before him. "I thank you, Grand Wizard, for allowing me to enter your wonderful home."

The wizard laughed, his hideous smile never fading. "Wonderful home, indeed," he said sarcastically. "It is nothing more than a dark, smelly cave." He spat on the floor. "In any case, I hope my specter-guard did not frighten you too much. It is there solely to test the bravery of those who seek me; it can cause no physical harm."

"I was not afraid of it, Oh Master of Magic."

"Of course not. You appear to be the sort of man who would not be deterred by such an apparition. Please be seated." The wizard motioned to the chair on the other side of the table. I sat down as he asked, "Why have you come here?"

"I seek your help, Grand Wizard."

His smile faded. "Of course. No one ever comes to a wizard unless they need help. Well, what is it? Do you need a love potion? Something to dispel demons? Enchanted armor?"

I shook my head. "What I need is not for my benefit, Wizard. You see, I am a humble soldier of King Hestate. His daughter recently turned sixteen, and he sent out a message throughout the land that all men of wealth and nobility would be allowed to come and try to win her love. The princess welcomed all suitors except one, an old man whose lips were dark as night. He had long jagged scars across his cheeks and forehead. His beady eyes were sunken into his shriveled, wrinkled face. His claw-like fingers were hard and black. The princess immediately turned him away before he made it across the drawbridge. What the princess did not know was that the man was the dark wizard Baskaf."

The wizard stroked his beard. "Yes. Dark magic causes the physical distortion of those who practice it." He chuckled. "No doubt Baskaf did not like being rejected by a mere mortal girl."

I nodded. "Baskaf used his powers to create a giant ice-monster called Zicern to freeze the castle and all who dwell inside. Now Baskaf resides in the icy palace, gazing upon the frozen beauty of the woman who refused to accept him."

"Why were you not frozen?"

"I was patrolling the nearby village when Zicern attacked the castle. I knew a direct assault against a magical creature would be foolish, so I came to you for help. I need a way to defeat Baskaf and free the princess."

The wizard grinned. "And is it your hope that by freeing the princess, she will take you as her husband?"

I felt my face blush. "Well... yes... I mean, no, I... that is not my primary concern. I only want to defeat Baskaf and restore peace to the kingdom."

The wizard got up from his seat and walked to the shelf of liquids. As he mixed several liquids in a jar, he said, "I take it this princess is quite beautiful, hmm?"

"Oh, indeed she is. Her hair is the color of golden sunshine, her eyes are as blue as the sea, her skin a silky white..." I stopped, for a moment picturing the glorious angelic vision of the princess. Then I shook myself back to reality. "But that is irrelevant. I just wish to defeat Baskaf and save the kingdom. It is my duty and responsibility as a soldier of King Hestate that I do so."

"Of course," the wizard chuckled. Then he stopped mixing the liquids and stared at the wall.

"What is the matter?" I asked.

He blinked his eyes. "Oh, I was just thinking." He faced me. "Did you know that I have never felt the touch of a woman? The only woman who has ever kissed me or let me touch her in any way was my mother. Never have I known what it is like to love or be loved."

I opened my mouth, but could think of nothing to say. How could I respond? And how was his random comment supposed to help me accomplish my task? These questions aggravated my anxiety, but I pushed this aside, for I knew I would have to be patient and endure the wizard's eccentricity for the sake of the princess.

The wizard went back to preparing the mixture. "Perhaps it is better this way. After all, who could ever love a creature such as myself?"

"Surely there is a woman who could love you, Grand Wizard. Perhaps you will find your one true love some day. After all, the world is filled with all sorts of people."

He shook his head. "I have turned my back on the world: Too much petty squabbling and deceit for my tastes. No, I prefer letting the people come to me. Perhaps one day a beautiful maiden will make the trek, and she will fall in love with me."

I frowned. How could he expect some woman to just walk in and declare her love for him? Did he not understand the complexities of love? Then I realized that if he had been hidden away in his cave for as long as people had said, his ideas of human behavior must have become distorted. He could understand the idea of love, but not its true meaning.

"Had the princess decided on a husband before she was frozen?" the wizard asked over his shoulder.

"No. None of the princes had been rich and handsome enough for her tastes."

He nodded, then filled a small vial with the green liquid he had created. He handed the vial and a piece of parchment to me. "Take these with you. Before you fight the monster, drink this potion and read aloud the first stanza of words on this parchment. After you have defeated him, speak the second stanza, which you must memorize before the battle."

I took the items. "Thank you, Grand Wizard. What do you ask as payment?"

The wizard opened his mouth to speak, but then stroked his beard in thought. "I always trust a client to pay me after my potion has served its purpose," he said. "You need not compensate me until after you defeat Baskaf and free the princess."

I stood, unfastened the small pouch of gold coins that hung from my belt, and threw it on the table.

"Take this for now," I said, then quickly ran out of the cave before he could respond.

* * *

A bitter breeze swept across the abandoned village that stood before the castle of King Hestate. The frigid air entered the forest where I sat atop my red, travel-weary horse, and seeped through my chain mail to chill my bones.

My heart ached, but not from the cold. I sighed mournfully at the sight of the ice-covered palace that I had kept watch over for so many years. Giant pointed pillars of ice—thirty feet wide and over one hundred feet tall—had sprung up where the large moat around the castle had been.

I balled my hand into a fist. "I will set things right." I dismounted from my steed and tied him to a tree. "Stay here," I instructed, and began walking through the village. Snow covered the roofs of the huts, and I trudged through the thick white layer that coated the ground. The villagers had all evacuated to the nearby hills and prayed that their land would be saved.

"I will save their land," I vowed. "I will rescue the princess, and all will be set right."

I heard a loud screech, like the sound of metal scrapping across rock, suddenly come from the vicinity of the castle. An immense being, nearly one hundred feet tall, stepped out from behind two of the icy pillars. It was Zicern, the ice-monster created by Baskaf. His trowel-shaped head hung even with his broad shoulders, which had dozens of mammoth icicles protruding from them. His thick forearms and large feet ended in long icy claws. Sharp, jagged icicles jutted from his elbows and knees. The monster stared at me with violet eyes and let out another screech from his fish-like mouth.

As soon as the monster saw me, I drank the tasteless potion. Then I opened the parchment and read aloud the first stanza. "Beast of evil, created from a dark wizard's desire, prepare to die when touched by the dragon's fire."

The vial and parchment disintegrated as a strange tingling sensation spread through my body. Suddenly, I began to rise off the ground. I quickly realized I was growing. I looked down to see huge sharp talons emerge from my boots. My chain mail became thick gray scales that spread across my arms and legs. A long tail emerged from the base of my spine, and my hands transformed into sharp scaly claws. My mouth and nose pushed away from my face to become a muzzle filled with sharp, twisted teeth. I felt a series of spines emerge from the top of my head, along my neck and back and down my tail.

"What the—" I growled, my voice suddenly deep and inhuman.

Zicern stared at me, momentarily confused. Then he let out a battle cry. I growled angrily and raced toward him. He opened his mouth, and a stream of icy liquid flew from it and struck me in the chest. I fell to the ground, my scales burning with cold. Zicern fired again, freezing my left shoulder to the ground. I struggled to get to my feet, but the stabbing pain of the ice was too much for me to handle.

As Zicern advanced toward me, I suddenly felt a bizarre change within myself. An uncontrollable, bestial rage enveloped my mind. At the same time, I felt a warm tingling at the bottom of my throat. It slowly became hotter and hotter as it climbed up into my mouth. I gagged, and a ball of orange fire flew from my open jaws and struck Zicern in the chest. The ice-monster stood, stunned, as his chest turned to water.

I looked down at the ice covering my body. I breathed a short flame over it, quickly melting it away. I got to my feet as Zicern broke off a chunk of ice from a nearby pillar and shoved it into his chest. His wound immediately healed, and he let out a screech of anger.

I got down on my hands and feet and charged, my huge talons ripping into the icy ground. I leapt into the air, smashing my spiked head into Zicern's chest. He fell back against a pillar. I tore off its icy summit and rammed it into his chest. Zicern grinned at me as the summit slowly melded with his chest. A sharp dagger of ice suddenly slid from his mouth and stabbed me in the side of my face. I fell to the ground, my face throbbing in pain. Blood seeped from the wound and froze on my jaw.

Zicern sprayed me with ice, cocooning me in a frozen shell. The coldness seeped through my thick scaly hide. I soon lost feeling throughout my body as the ice closed over my head. Then the beast started applying a second layer of ice over me.

I growled in anger. I was not going to allow some cursed ice-monster to prevent me from liberating the princess and taking her as my bride! My rage became a burning fire within me. The heat swelled in my throat, and I forced it into my stomach. From there it spread to my arms, legs, and tail. The tremendous heat in my torso and limbs began to melt away the ice, and I regained feeling in my body. I let the heat surge up my throat and into my mouth, from which I spat a fireball. It burst through my icy container and struck Zicern in the face. He screeched in pain as I broke free of the melting ice cocoon.

I leapt to my feet and swung around, striking Zicern with my tail and knocking him to the ground. I then blasted away at him with fire. Streams of water flowed from his dissolving body as he started to melt away. His left arm suddenly lunged forward, his claws sinking into my right leg. Blood sprang from the wound and instantly froze on my scales. I bent down and spewed a wide flame across Zicern's limb, immediately turning it to water. I blasted my icy opponent in the chest and belly. He let out a long, high-pitched scream of pain as the rest of his body quickly changed to water.

I stepped back, examining my opponent. Zicern was now nothing more than a misshapen pile of icy mush.

I turned my attention to the castle, where the drawbridge had suddenly lowered. The front doors flew open, and a dark figure emerged. Baskaf looked at the remains of Zicern, then up at me.

"You wretch! You have killed Zicern, one of my favorite creations." He walked toward me. "Why have you come here?"

"To free the princess," I grunted, hating the sound of my own voice.

Baskaf gave out an eerie, hollow cackle. "You don't understand what I have done, do you?"

"You have taken the princess and everyone in the castle hostage!"

Baskaf frowned. "I know that I possess many traits that you mortals consider vile, but vanity is not one of them. I could have easily come here disguised as the richest, most handsome man in the world. But instead I chose to appear as I really am. And the princess refused to see me." His voice became a sinister rasp. "She could have had a powerful wizard as her husband, but she gave up that chance when she refused to see me because I am homely!" He motioned toward the castle. "Now she will pay for judging people by their appearances! Her icy entombment will serve as an example to all like her!"

"No!" I stomped my foot, turning the ice beneath it into broken mush. "I will set her free!"

Baskaf shook his head. "I know you are nothing more than a human who has used magic to become a dragon. I will easily destroy you." He raised his hands to the sky. "Behold the power of Baskaf!"

Black lightning sizzled from his fingertips and covered his body. He began to grow as his black robe melted into a layer of dark skin. His fingers became long tendrils covered with sharp barbs. Bristly fur covered his arms and legs, as plates of bony armor appeared on his back. His lower legs thickened and split into six black tendrils. His mouth became round and leech-like and was filled with rows of sharp pointed teeth. His eyes changed into glossy, ebony spheres. Six long spines grew from behind his head.

My monstrous rage intensified as Baskaf transformed. "You have imprisoned my beloved," I said, "and for that, you must die!"

Baskaf hissed, and I growled back. He took a step toward me. I lunged forward just as he leapt straight into the air and came down on my back. His immense weight forced me to my knees. His barbed tendrils wrapped around my arms and neck. He reached his head over my shoulder and sank his teeth into my soft underbelly, from which he began to drain the blood from my body.

My muscles screamed in protest as I tried to stand. I quickly fell forward, sending Baskaf crashing face-first into the ice. He released his grip, and I pulled away from him. I got to my feet, fire building in my throat. Baskaf also stood, hissing loudly and waving his tendrils in a menacing manner. Two tendrils shot forward and wrapped around my upper jaw, then forced it upward. Another tendril slid into my throat and forced itself down my windpipe. This caused me to gag, and the now-flaming tendril instantly pulled out of my mouth. I snapped my jaw shut, sending sharp serrated teeth through the other tendrils. I opened my maw enough to allow the bloody limbs to retreat back to their owner.

I smiled, completely confident that victory was mine. Baskaf's eyes turned red with anger as he read my expression. His tendrils lashed out again, tripping me. As I fell I fired another fireball that struck him in the neck. He screamed as his flesh was incinerated. I clenched one of his tendrils and pulled myself toward him. He grabbed a large chunk of ice and used it to club my head. I blasted the ice with fire, then leapt up and plunged my claws into his mouth, forcing it open. I let loose a stream of fire that soared down his throat and into his body. Baskaf tried to scream in pain, but his throat had been reduced to ashes. He swayed for a moment, smoke spewing from his mouth, his open eyes seeing nothing. I gave him a light push, using my tail. He fell backward onto the watery remains of Zicern.

I reared back and let out a roar of triumph. Then I used my flames to heat the air around the castle. The ice on its walls crackled and shattered. The water from the melting ice pillars began to fill the moat.

I fell to my knees, my whole body throbbing, pain swelling in my bloody wounds. I said the second stanza on the parchment, which I had quickly memorized before the battle. "Evil has been purged from this land. Return this dragon to the form of a man."

I started to shrink. I felt my tail retract into my body and my scaly skin become my chain mail. The spines on my back withered and seeped back into my skin. Even before the transformation was complete, I was on my weary feet and racing toward the castle. I rushed across the drawbridge, passed through the open doors, raced up an immense flight of wide stairs, and flung open the door to the princess's chamber.

There she lay upon her bed, water streaming from her petite body. Her beauty radiated from her like steam. I rushed to her side, my heart leaping in my chest. I slowly knelt down and kissed her full, luscious lips.

She slowly lifted her eyelids. She blinked, then looked at me with shimmering blue eyes.

And screamed.

"Guards! GUARDS!"

"Princess—" I started, then quickly covered my mouth. Had that growl come from me?

The princess squirmed to the other side of the bed, the covers drawn over her for protection, her eyes wide with fear. "Guards, help me! There's a monster in my bed chamber!"

I looked to my left, and caught sight of my reflection in the full-length mirror on the wall.

The next scream I heard was my own.

My pupils were reptilian slits. My hair had been replaced by a cover of thick gray scales and bony knobs. My nostrils clung close to my face. My mouth was full of pointed, gnarled teeth. I put my hand to my face, and realized its fingers had become sharp, scaly talons.

I raced from the chamber, the princess still screaming for the guards. I ran down the stairs, almost slipping in the water that covered them. I flew out the doors and fell into a gigantic puddle. I sloshed my way out of it, and then raced across the drawbridge. I slipped and painfully fell to my hands and knees, so I continued to flee by crawling. I collapsed by the side of one of the huts in the village. Tears poured from my inhuman eyes and down my hideous face. My mind worked furiously, trying to figure out what had happened to me.

Then I heard a horse neigh. I looked up to see a figure emerge from the forest. He was dressed in shimmering silver garments. He wore golden boots and gauntlets, and a golden cape hung from his well-muscled neck. Curls of golden hair encircled his face, which contained bright blue eyes and a perfectly sculpted nose. He rode a large white stallion with reigns of silver and a saddle of gold.

I watched him pass through the village, the snow melting beneath his horse's hooves. He stopped in front of me and smiled. His teeth were bright white, and all perfectly aligned. I looked away to avoid being blinded by their radiance.

He tossed something to me, which I caught with my talons. It was the pouch of gold I had given to the wizard at the mountain.

"That is to pay for your horse," he said, patting his steed. I looked at the horse's dark eyes, and realized that it was indeed my horse, yet somehow changed into the glorious creature it was now. The man looked at the castle. "Now I will collect my payment for the magical potion and parchment. But first, allow me to thank you for destroying Baskaf. I would have done it myself but I did not wish to risk my life fighting a powerful dark wizard."

"What have you done to me?" I demanded, my words almost completely lost in a series of growls.

He laughed, and I felt chills run up and down my spine. "Just eliminated your chances of becoming the princess's husband. I created the spell to transform you into a dragon, but to not fully change you back into a man."

"Why?" I asked in despair.

"It is quite simple. Talking with you convinced me that it was time to pursue my destiny. For too long I have used my powers to help others, but not myself. Why should I, a master of magic, live in a dark, smelly cave while you mortal fools dwell in majestic castles? I think it is time I settle down with someone who is worthy of my time and affection. Someone with hair like golden sunshine and eyes as blue as the sea."

I let out a savage cry and leapt at him. He calmly waved his hand, and some invisible force pulled my body to the wet ground.

"Now, now, dragon-man, you must behave yourself. In time, when I become king, you may wish to seek employment as one of my guards." He smiled. "After all, I'll need someone to protect me from evil wizards." He laughed as his newly acquired steed carried him toward the castle.

Space Leviathans

They have inhabited the heavens
Since the beginning of time.
These magnificent creatures
Larger as planets, their tails
As long as the Kuiper Belt unraveled.

Sleek as hawks they glide,
Darker than night,
Breathing the same vacuum
That exsanguinates us.
Flat space leviathans.

Their eyes the size
Of the American continent,
Congealed with stray asteroids
Flicked into their eyes
During flight.

They migrate
Once in 12,500 Earth years,
Sweeping past our galaxy.
A cyclone spinning through
A little Kansas town.

In their wake, planet orbits reverse.
The smaller ones explode on impact,
Leaving a trail of asteroids
Specks in their eyes.
The Mayans charted their return.

— Christina Sng

HOKEY POKEY

By Ken Goldman

"Well, lookin' back on it, I'd guess the idea must've seemed a bit crazy even to a couple of youngsters. But it was just kids bein' kids, you know, and sometimes boys get caught up in the moment, when doin' what's crazy seems like the only thing to do..."

Eliajah Woodman, age 73
Caretaker of Mt. Mariah Cemetery

Jordy sat with Tag upon the rusted porch swing behind the old farmhouse. A brisk wind tousled the older boy's hair, its chill an unwelcome forecast of the winter to come. "Did you forget what today is?" he asked his kid brother.

Tag focused on the thickening clouds riding the bleeding autumn sky. "Nope. I didn't forget it's Dad's birthday. There's not much point to remembering, though, is there?"

The younger boy had not spoken much about his father during the past few months, but his brother had caught him crying in his room on more than one occasion. Jordy had taken the death even worse. Dead parents have the nasty tendency to haunt their sons, and more than a year after severe cardiac failure had claimed Elliott Darnell, his father's death seemed to be all the boy talked about.

"How old would Dad have been?" Tag asked.

"Don't know. Old."

Jordy would not let the topic drop until he had explored new territory yielding fresh explanations of a universe that had done this to him. Recently he had difficulty remembering details of his dad's face, and even the sound of his voice was slipping away. He worried that maybe soon there would be nothing left.

"You ever think about what he looks like under the ground, Tag? If Dad looks the same, the way we remember him?"

The sun was descending behind the western hills and Tag seemed reluctant to take his attention from the sky, as if some precious moment might be lost. He hesitated before his eyes found his brother's.

"That's a weird thing to be thinking about. There's a decent sunset this evening. Why not let's just watch it?"

The older boy allowed the sky's palate of colors to carry him to some other place, but the distraction did not last. No October twilight could rival the shadowy denizens lurking inside.

"Your father is dead Jordy, and his rotting corpse is alone and unloved, stinking in his grave…"

"I've just been wondering, is all. Maybe bugs got into his coffin. Maybe he's still wearing those damned horned rimmed glasses over empty holes where his eyes were."

"We buried him wearing those horned rims, didn't we? I don't think Dad took them off after we put him into the ground. It's his birthday, so I'd rather not think about insects crawling out of his sockets, okay?"

The older boy kept silent for a moment. So much about death made no sense. Where was the logic behind placing eyeglasses on his dead father's face the day of the funeral? Tag had mentioned this was just a way to make his corpse more closely resemble the living man his family had known, but wasn't this a lie that made death seem like something it wasn't?

"—stinking in his grave—"

Jordy hated these dark passages through which his thinking lead him. He dug deep for one of the good memories.

"You remember that song he used to sing with us, Tag? The one he taught us how to do with our hands and feet?"

"—and our asses? That stupid Hokey Pokey song? How could I forget?"

He sang a few words under his breath.

"You put your right foot in, you put your right foot out. You put your right foot in, and you…"

The memory of a birthday party washed over Jordy. He and a dozen friends had entangled themselves in a riotous knot during his dad's quickening Hokey Pokey lyrics and motions. Everyone was laughing; some kids were even falling down. It was a wonderful moment, one worth remembering. But he had almost forgotten.

"A piece of Dad's soul might still be buried with him, you know. Something must be left of him the bugs can't get to. Something not flesh and bone."

Tag's eyebrow raised in that skeptic's fashion that informed you that you were full of shit. "What's with Dad is dirt and worms, maggots, cockroaches, and slugs! Maybe some skin is left, like a chewed up dog bone, but that's all. Shit, Jordy! You're going on fifteen. That's almost two years older than me. Use your damned head!"

Tag's few glimpses at anything dead consisted of the roadkill they occasionally discovered out on the highway. Once he had complained that death was bloody and it smelled bad. The night their dad had collapsed at dinner the guys who came with the ambulance just tossed a sheet over his body as if what lay under were too awful to look at.

"Well, I think his soul is still down there... or *somewhere*. I think there's more to being dead than just worms and dog bones, Tag. I don't know exactly what's left, but there's someone who's looking after Dad, making sure he's okay." Saying this did not make Jordy fully believe it, but the words helped. "Maybe you feel like going up to Mt. Mariah with me to find out? I mean, just so we can know what's what?"

The words just came out, Jordy didn't know from where. Maybe he had been waiting to speak them all along. He expected his kid brother to respond with shock or disbelief over his suggestion with all its grisly implications, maybe calling him a regal asshole for even mentioning it. But Tag seemed curious.

"You mean dig him up?"

"Just to be sure."

"Take Dad out of the ground?"

"That's what I'm saying."

"Now let me get this straight. You're telling me we should just hike up to that ol' bone yard with shovels right now and disturb Dad's grave?"

"Uh huh."

Tag took a moment as if testing the depths of his own conscience.

"You know how wrong that is? Mom would kill us."

"It's Friday. Ladies Night at The Buck-Eye. Mom won't even know."

Jordy hoped the same pre-pubescent demon that had spoken for him might whisper to his brother.

"Well, why not? Why the hell not? You want to know, don't you? Just like when you sneak a peek at those roadkill cats smeared like bloody pancakes..."

"Maybe I'll just go up there with you to see you do it. 'Cause I know you're just talkin' the talk and you won't do it, Jordy. Not in a billion years."

"Well, we won't know about that 'till we get there, will we?"

"This is so wrong..."

"Maybe. Maybe not."

The brothers shook on it, demonstrating their honorable intentions were not the least bit contaminated with the curiosity that a dead father's remains would look pretty ripe after so many months. That would be a terrible reason to hike up to the old Mt. Mariah graveyard using their father's own tool shed shovels to do the job.

You had to respect the dead. But you had to know the truth too.

Dad deserved that much.

* * *

The last trace of daylight had abandoned the sky as the brothers approached Mt. Mariah's rear entrance. Each tossed a shovel over the high iron gate that surrounded the old bone yard. Climbing a nearby oak, they scaled the barrier. Roving shadows played mindfuck games as the boys searched the jagged rows of headstones for their father's burial site. Although the grass was freshly manicured, a cemetery becomes a different place at night. Its amenities went unnoticed in the uncertain moonlight as the boys wandered the lumpy grounds amid the tombstones.

Finally the familiar inscription appeared:

Elliott P. Darnell
October 20, 1953 - August 19, 1999
Beloved Husband and Father

"You're okay with this?" Jordy asked. "'Cause once we start, there's no changing your mind."

"I'm okay," Tag said, but he didn't sound like he was.

The older brother broke ground first. Tag needed a moment to digest the significance of their act, then set himself to the task. Together the two attacked the earth made soft by a recent gully washer. One brother eyed the other, each seeking silent encouragement, a voiceless agreement that what they were doing would not ram them both directly into hell.

After an hour's work Jordy broke the silence first. "*You put your left hand in, you put your left hand out. You put your left hand in, and you shake it all about...*"

Keeping his voice low Tag joined him, and they sang as they shoveled, prodding out clods of damp earth in time to the rhythm.

"*...You do the hokey pokey then you turn yourself around. That's what it's all about!*"

Laughing, the brothers headed into another chorus with more enthusiasm.

"*You put your right hand in, you put your right hand out. You put your right hand in, and you—*"

Jordy's shovel struck something solid. Each looked to the other in the night's stillness. Something vibrated beneath their feet. It wasn't much, but for one terrible moment the brothers froze where they stood.

"***...and you... shake it... all about...***"

Standing inside the deep hole Jordy looked to Tad for confirmation of what he had heard.

[You?]

His brother shrugged.

[Not me...]

In the darkness they could feel the edge of the coffin's lid through the dirt below. Tag attempted a forced smile that aborted itself at once. He tried whispering but could only gasp his next words.

"Let's put both our feet the hell out of this hole, okay? And I'm not talking about the hokey pokey, Jordy."

His brother's remark made the older boy break into

convulsed laughter. Tag was no match for the moment's heebie-jeebies, and along with his brother shook so hard with his own nervous cackling he had to hold his stomach to keep from losing his dinner.

The soft dirt beneath quivered. Something seemed to shift its weight as if the soil had heaved and swelled. The thick mud made solid footing tricky and it was difficult to tell.

"He's right below us. We can do this, Tag, but we have to do it together. Are you with me?"

"Let's just leave while we still—"

But the older boy already had decided. He crouched to his knees moving closer to the sunken casket, then looked back to Tag.

"It's only Dad under here, you know."

He returned to the song in the manner that it was meant to be sung, slowly, the way he had heard his father at weddings and birthday parties.

"*You-put-your-left-leg-in, you-put-your-left-leg-out, You-put-your-left-leg-in, and-you-shake-it-all-about…*"

Jordy nodded for his brother to help him out. The younger boy's lips moved, but no words came. He had better luck with his second attempt. Together they managed a shaky rendition of the next line.

"*You do… the hokey pokey… and you shake it all about...*"

Jordy shoveled great clumps of sticky earth from the casket. Taking his brother's cue, Tag did the same. When the entire top portion of the pinewood box appeared, Jordy maneuvered his ear close to the lid as if eavesdropping on a conversation.

"I think something's moving inside. Listen."

Tag followed his brother's instruction, kneeling in the soft mud closer to the coffin.

"I don't hear anything. Maybe it's just bugs. Or rats."

"Listen better, twerp! I'm telling you there's something moving in there!"

Tag's ear brushed the cheap knotted pine of the coffin's lid. The wood was not especially thick, and he pressed his cheek against it to hear if there was anything.

"Jordy, I swear if you're fucking with me…"

Tag suddenly pulled his face away from the pinewood and jumped, falling backwards. He skittered as far as he could propel himself in reverse while on his ass.

"I heard a thump. Christ, Jordy, I think he's trying to push the top open! I just felt him hit the goddamn lid!"

"Can you see anything? I can't tell. It's too—"

The coffin's hinges creaked. Its top might have slipped a bit over the lip then fell back again with a thud, but in the darkness nothing seemed certain. The rusted metal of the hinges moaned one more time and this time the lid gave way. A sudden breeze kicked up, carrying with it the stench of rotted meat.

[—*alone and stinking in his grave, Jordy—stinking in his grave—*]

"D-Dad?" Jordy managed.

"Right foot... in... right foot... out..."

"I think he's sitting up, Jordy—I think he's..."

"I can't tell—it's too dark to see any —"

Something landed in Jordy's lap, and he held it close to his face to examine. The night did not permit a clear view, but touching the object left no doubt. He handed it to his brother.

"His glasses?" Tag asked.

"I think so. Yes, I think—"

"...you do... the... hokey pokey..."

Tag dropped the horned-rims into the mud.

"I want to go, Jordy. I want to get the hell out of here now!"

"Not yet..." The older boy leaned close to the coffin and whispered, "It's us, Dad. Tag and Jordy."

"Christ, Jordy!"

"We just wanted to say happy birthday, Dad."

"Oh shit, Jordy! Let's just—"

"I'm way ahead of you, Tagger."

Jordy climbed out of the hole first, pulling his brother free. From below, he heard another gurgling attempt at speech.

"That's... what it's... all about... all... about..."

The older boy took a last look into the opened grave trying to determine something, anything. The darkness would not permit it.

Finally he said, "We're going now, Dad." He looked to his brother.

Tag hesitated, then stepped closer to the hole.

"See ya'."

They ran all the way home.

* * *

The expected phone call came early in the morning. Some old guy asking to speak to Florence Darnell identified himself as Eliajah Woodman, the caretaker at Mt. Mariah, and he mentioned how the grave belonging to her late husband had been vandalized during the night.

Finding answers did not require astute detective work. The brothers had dragged sludge into the kitchen while layers of dried muck saturated their clothing. The two insisted they had been mud wrestling near the pond, but the old guy on the phone had another shoe to drop. He had found shovels inside their father's opened grave, and the initials E.P.D. carved into the handles provided smoking gun evidence. The boys admitted what they had done, but there seemed no sane reason to tell what they had seen. They had pissed off enough people already.

Their mother was among them, but her anger didn't last long. The tears did, and old Eliajah had to soften his own anger considerably to prevent the young widow from becoming outright hysterical.

"They're just kids bein' kids, is all," Woodman remarked, and he asked the woman to go easy on her two boys. The old guy assured her no permanent damage had been done and that he had no desire to pursue the matter further. He asked if he might have a moment to speak to the older boy.

Florence Darnell held out the receiver for her son. Lip synching a feeble "I'm sorry, Mom," the boy approached the phone as if she were handing him a dead rat.

"Is this Jordy I'm speakin' to?" Eliajah asked.

"Yes, sir…"

"It's only us two on the line, is that so, son?"

"Yes, sir."

"That's good, son, that's real good. Now just in case your mama is in the room, I want you to keep 'Yes Sirring' me and listenin' real good. You hear me talkin' to you, Jordy?"

"Uh huh... sir."

"That was a real terrible thing you and your brother done last night. But you already know that much, so that's not what this is about. I want you listenin' to me now like you ain't never listened to nobody before. I mean with both ears turned to high volume."

"Yes..."

"All right, then, here it is. You ain't gonna do no more grave visitin' on my shift, son. You and your kid brother is gonna keep off Mt. Mariah's grounds 'cept durin' reg'lar visitin' hours, or I'll show you some real hokey pokey. And *that's* what it's all about..."

The old man cackled like a mad elf. His voice suddenly seemed oddly familiar.

"Now put your mama back on the phone, Boy, so we can wrap this damned mess up proper."

Within minutes Jordy had fastened the lock inside his room for the first time since his father's funeral. He knew a lecture was coming, but for now he had something inside his head that demanded serious reflection. His brain replayed the same scene like a rewound video.

...Eliajah Woodman discovers two boys digging up a grave and he hears them muttering some shit about the hokey pokey. The damage has already been done to Elliott P. Darnell's plot, so the old fart is just goosing up a little payback for himself by scaring the bejeezus out of the vandals who have had the balls to ravage the grounds he's responsible for. The geezer hides himself behind a nearby headstone and throws his voice in the dark like one of those old-time ventriloquists working with a dummy, knowing how the dark plays mean tricks on a couple of spooked kids whose imaginations are already into hyperdrive. Old Eliajah laughs himself sick watching the two vandals practically fudge their pants.

It was a stretch, of course, but who could say it didn't happen that way? Jordy hadn't seen anything he could swear to, and Tag was just a kid who watched too many vampire movies. This revised version made a whole lot more sense than a dead man climbing out of his coffin to do the hokey pokey did. No, Dad wasn't trapped inside that pinewood box. His soul was floating around somewhere in heaven, looking down on both him and Tag, safe with Jesus and his angels while God watched over him. Hell, this was what everyone else believed, wasn't it? What lay beneath the dirt at Mt. Mariah wasn't really his dad. Not any more.

So why even bother giving a second thought about where those dumb-ass horned rimmed glasses came from?

Or that awful smell...

* * *

Eliajah Woodman held a pair of eyeglasses as he spoke to the woman on the phone. He did not especially like nodding and smiling like an idiot, but the words he uttered called for it.

"Yes, I think we can put the matter behind us, Mrs. Darnell. I wouldn't go too hard on your boys. In time I'm sure both Jordy and Tag will come to understand what they did was just an expression of the grief any youngster feels for a lost parent. You take care now."

Woodman returned the phone to its cradle, and removing a ragged kerchief from his hip pocket he mopped sweat from his brow. It had been a long night and there was work to be done at the Darnell plot. The diggers would be arriving any time now to put things back the way they were, so he would have to be quick.

"Fuckin' kids..."

He studied the horned rims in his hands. Those damned eyeglasses came close to causing him some nasty trouble. He would have to be more careful about falling asleep so early during his shift.

"I guess you'll be wantin' these specs returned before the diggers get here. Must've fallen off your face durin' all that excitement, eh? I've got to put you back where you belong. I'm sorry, Elliott. Happy birthday."

He handed the horned rims to the rotting corpse that sat inside his small office.

Eliott P. Darnell indeed wanted his glasses.

He put his right hand out...

I Saw the Dead

Marching to the bathroom
In the dark of night
I saw the dead

They looked at me
From the end of the hallway
"What are you doing in my hall?" I ask.

"It's not a hall, it's an interdimensional portal
to ancient Egypt," the ghosts replied.
"O.K., whatever—I have to go to the bathroom," I mumbled,
and fumbled for the light switch.

Relieved; I turned to see if they were still there, but only a
dim glowing hole in my hallway remained—
a doorway to Egypt perhaps?

Back in bed, recreating perfect spooned symmetry
Between my sweet Laura's butt and the edge of my bed—
Drifting off into sleep, wondering,
"What's an interdimensional portal doing outside my bathroom?

— Charles P. Ries

THE GARDEN OF SYR

By Mark Anthony Brennan

"So this is all I need?" asked Sol, placing the filter mask on his face.

"Yes. And you only need it out here on the plain. The air in the city's fine," said Karlson. He was already wearing his mask. Although it covered the entire lower part of his face, the mask was transparent except for the wafer-thin filter over his right cheek. "Even out here, you only need it in the evening when the gases below the surface are released into the air."

"So, when will they see me?"

Sol was anxious—he was dying to see the legendary Mirona City. With the planet being isolated from the Federation, stories of the city were almost mythical. A beautiful place with elegant architecture, they'd say, where culture and the arts thrive.

And if Mirona City was a sparkling jewel then it was truly a diamond in the rough—it sat on the most barren piece of rock in colonized space.

"You'll see them soon enough. Don't worry. You're on Mirona now. You have to do things their way."

Sol sighed and looked around the room. "In the meantime, I get to share these deluxe accommodations with you. Is that it?"

"Look, it's a violation of the Strasbourg Treaty that you're here right now," said Karlson, leaning back in his chair. "Would you rather I contacted the Feds and tell them you're here?"

Sol looked Karlson over. *Who is this joker anyway?*

Karlson wore an old soiled and tattered flight suit. It clearly wasn't functional, so it could only serve to remind people that he was an ex-spacer. As if the shack's décor wasn't clue enough. Chunks of a spaceship hull were imbedded in the walls in various places like so many pieces of visual art. An instrumentation panel lined one wall, and most of the furniture in the room—the tables, the chairs, even the door—were relics from a space vessel.

Sol looked up at the speakers in the ceiling above them. *What the hell is that? Sounds like someone dumping a load of cutlery onto a metal floor.*

"You like that?" Eyes closed, Karlson's head swayed back and forth to the rhythm of the music. "It's splang music. Ever heard it?"

Splang? Last time I heard that was in some dive on New Earth fifty years ago. It was out of style then.

"Yeah, great. So what's the deal. You're the Federation's ambassador or something?"

"Special Consul, man."

Special Consul. Excuse me.

"Well, let's just keep the Feds out of this," said Sol. "I'm here as a legitimate trader. I'm sure the Mironites would like to do business."

Karlson stopped swaying his head to the music and sat up straight in his chair. His face was haggard, creased with the lines of age. His eyes looked tired. "Why'd you come here anyway? Don't you know their history?"

"I know as much as the next guy. Formerly a Federation mining outpost. They had some kind of religious caste system—only the higher caste could marry, hold office and stuff. That's where they ran into problems with the Fed's anti-discrimination laws. They finally couldn't tolerate having rules dictated by the Fed and declared independence." Sol gave a short laugh. "It would have been a bigger deal if this place had any significance whatsoever."

"You should have more respect, my friend." Karlson turned his head towards the shack's window. Several hundred meters away, across the purple-tinted landscape, sat a large, squat cylinder. Sol's ship. "What are you carryin'?"

"With the trade embargo, I figured that the Mironites would be anxious to see anything from the outside world."

Karlson looked Sol steadily in the eyes. "*What*, exactly?"

"I've had enough of this," said Sol. His flight suit rustled as he stood up. "You are the one that contacted me and requested me to land here. How do I know you have the authority? What's to stop me from just walking over there?" He jerked his head in the direction the city.

Karlson shrugged. "They don't give me a badge or anything. But believe me, all contact with the Federation, including traders like you, goes through me. That's why I'm here."

"Yeah, why *are* you here?" Sol waved his arm, indicating the makeshift shack around them. "You're just a stone's throw from one of the most beautiful cities around. Why do you live here?"

"There are reasons," growled Karlson. "Now let's get back to your cargo…"

"Fuck this, pal. I'm going over there. I'll take my chances."

Sol stormed out of the old spacer's shack and strode off in the direction of Mirona City. Less than two kilometers away, the city was clearly visible—its slender towers and spires glowing a brilliant orange as they caught the light of the setting sun.

The brittle, purple rock crunched under Sol's feet. Despite the lateness of the day, it was still hot out on the plain. Although his flight suit insulated his body, Sol could feel the heat on his exposed head.

He had only taken few steps when there came a low rumbling sound from behind, like distant thunder. Sol stopped in his tracks.

Christ, what the hell is that?

"You shouldn't be out here alone."

Sol gave a start. He hadn't noticed Karlson coming quietly up behind him.

"What is that?"

"Rolling rocks time, my friend. Ya see, out there towards the mountains," Karlson jerked his thumb back towards the direction of the shack, "the rocks in the planet's crust are already cooling. This whole plain has pockets of subterranean gases that are still hot from the day's heat. Right about now they start pushing up on the rock above that is starting to contract."

Sol squinted as he stared out across the plain behind them. Many kilometers away the squat, tangerine-colored sun was just sinking behind the mountains of Damas. On this side of the mountain range there was nothing but the vast, flat Plain of Syr.

"The city's OK, but once you've seen it, you've seen it," said Karlson. "I feel more at home out here. I was born on the prairies, you know. Alberta. Ever heard of it?"

"Never been to Earth," muttered Sol. *And I never will, pal.* There were several warrants out on Sol. Stepping foot on Federation Capital Territory would mean his immediate arrest.

"This reminds me a bit of home," said Karlson. "The flats, the distant mountains. Course, the colors are all wrong."

Sol surveyed the freakish landscape. The plain was completely flat, a nearly even carpet of purple rock. Above, the setting orb of burnt orange sat in a milky white sky. Wrong colors, indeed.

"And," continued Karlson, "nothin' grows out here. Weird, isn't it?" he asked, glancing over at Sol. "The air's breathable, but nothin' grows. Nothin'. Well, 'cept my garden that is."

"You have a garden?"

"That's what I call it." Before Sol could question him further Karlson started off, heading in the direction of the city. "We'd better get going," he called over his shoulder. "It'll soon be show time."

"So you'll take me? To the city?" asked Sol hurrying to catch up. There was more rumbling from the rolling rocks behind them.

"Yeah, sure. I'll show you the garden. It's on the way."

* * *

"These are incredible," whispered Sol.

It was a beautiful but eerie scene. Placed on the rocky flats, part way between the shack and the city, were a collection of statues. There were more than a hundred of them—men, women, children. Some were smiling; others had their mouths open as if in awe. Each statue was draped in a white flowing cloth, which gave the figures the appearance of angels—joyful, adoring angels.

"You did these?"

Karlson nodded. "Yeah. This is my garden."

The figures came in a startling array of colors. A few were almost black they were so dark, while others were bright colors—blue and green. Still others were streaked with various hues—red with yellow and brown, brown with green and purple. But the eyes were all the same. There were no pupils, irises or whites. They were just red. A translucent red—almost glowing.

Sol peered closely at the figure closest to him. It was a young man with his arms outstretched before him. He had a half-smile on his bright blue face. Despite the eyes and the outrageous coloring, the figure looked very life-like. The detail was incredible.

Sol touched the cheek of the statue. It was rock hard.

The statue behind the young man was of a middle-aged woman. She was kneeling with her hands clasped to her chest. Beneath the light robe the figure was a brilliant turquoise mottled with gray splotches. Again the detail was remarkable. The woman was staring upwards in rapture. Her mouth formed a joyful "O", as if she had witnessed something of startling beauty.

"They have no hair," said Sol. "None of them have hair."

"That's the Mironite style. They have no body hair. They consider it unappealing and unhygienic."

Sol looked over at Karlson as the sound of the rolling rocks got louder and closer. Karlson had long, greasy-looking hair with streaks of gray in it.

"What about your hair?"

"Oh, I'm not a Mironite. I'll never be one." Karlson started walking again through row upon row of angelic figures. The figures all faced the setting sun, as if that was the source of their joy.

"They won't let you in, will they?" asked Sol. He was keeping pace with Karlson, although occasionally a figure or two would get between the two men. "They keep you out here. It's that caste thing, right?"

"Yeah, that's part of it." Karlson stopped to adjust the clothing on the statue of a young woman. As with the others her light robe hung loosely around her shoulder and was fastened in front around her waist, like a tunic. As Karlson fussed with the material a few of the other white robes fluttered as a light breeze picked up. The breeze was cool.

The temperature drops quickly out here.

The rumbling of the rolling rocks was constant now. Sol had to raise his voice to speak.

"Part of it? What else?"

"It was punishment, mostly. You see the whole reason they're independent is that they are conscientious objectors. Their religion prohibits violence. And then I show up. An arms smuggler." Karlson looked over with a sheepish grin. "Pretty stupid, huh? I didn't do my homework. I figured they'd have some civil wars or underground crime."

"So you brought instruments of destruction to a society that abhors violence?" Sol was inwardly laughing at the irony. "Couldn't you get away?"

"Nah. I wrecked my ship when I landed." Karlson had moved on and was fussing with another statue. "Besides, I don't mind it here."

The last rays of the setting sun were casting long shadows in Karlson's garden of angels. Being evenly spaced and arranged, the statues were like trees in a carefully cultivated orchard. A hundred trees of stone growing up from a bed of purple rock. Sol felt dizzy as the strangeness of it all hit him. The scene had a dream-like quality.

"I don't understand. What's to like? They treat you like…"

"They should have killed me," said Karlson sharply. "To the Mironites, mine was the worst of all possible crimes. But they didn't kill me. They're more compassionate than that. They set me up out here. It worked out well for everyone."

"Everyone?"

"Yeah. The Feds don't like Mirona's discriminatory ways, so they isolate them—prohibit any contact with Fed citizens. That's what the Treaty is really all about. But then after a while the Feds realized there was value in maintaining some form of relations. So they were actually happy to have a contact person here on Mirona. The Feds even send me a small stipend."

The rumbling noise was getting louder. Sol could actually feel the ground vibrating under his feet. He looked back towards the mountains. The sun had just disappeared. In the distance there were columns rising from the floor of the plain. Smoke?

Sol turned around to find that Karlson had wandered off, still heading towards the city.

"Don't you get lonely?" asked Sol catching up to Karlson. With Mirona's gravity Sol's weight was close to fifty percent above normal. Any exertion made him a little breathless. That's probably why Karlson looked so old and worn—this heavy planet must literally drag him down.

"Not really. I had a wife, you know."

"Really?"

"Yeah, well not really a wife. I mean they wouldn't let us marry. In fact, they took her away after a while."

"That's barbarous. How do you…"

"Look," said Karlson, stopping and turning to face Sol. They had reached the edge of the garden. The orchard of red-eyed angels was behind them. Ahead of them, only a few hundred meters across the flats, were the delicate buildings of Mirona City. "*We* are the evil ones here, not them. We are the ones that bring in the crap from the outside world."

Before Sol could respond there was an explosion followed by a loud hissing sound. A geyser had erupted about a kilometer away. A long, thin plume of smoky green vapor shot several hundred meters into the air. In the failing light Sol could see several other geysers erupting here and there across the rumbling plain.

"What the fuck?"

"The city sits on a shield—a thick plate of dense rock." Karlson was almost yelling to be heard over the noise of the explosions. Geysers were continuously erupting in the direction of the mountains. "So the city is safe. There's a smaller shield below us, so it's safe here too. But all around us," Karlson waved his arms in a sweeping motion, "the rock layer isn't strong enough. When it cools—kaboom! The hot gases below force their way out. It's the same every night."

"Wow. That's something."

The ground was now shaking wildly. The Plain of Syr was alive as the green gas columns popped up everywhere.

"Why do you think I'm evil, Mr. Karlson?"

"Because I know what you're dealing, my friend," shouted Karlson. "There's only one commodity that anyone ever brings here anymore. Pleasure taps."

"Well, I… er…" stammered Sol.

"Don't bother denying it." Karlson narrowed his eyes. "These people didn't know what to make of the tap when you people first arrived. I mean, an electronic insert that stimulates your pleasure center? It seemed decadent but they saw nothing immoral in it. Why would they? They knew nothing of its addictive qualities. Not like I do."

"Look, Karlson, gimme a break here. It's just business. Why do you care? The way they treat you, why do you care?"

"Look out there, my friend," yelled Karlson pointing out towards the plain.

Sol looked. The explosions were deafening—it was like a battlefield out there. It was frightening. But it was exhilarating at the same time. The noise and the shaking excited him. And the sight of the towering plumes of gas was glorious.

"It's beautiful!"

"Yes, it is," bellowed Karlson. "And when you're on the tap it's irresistible. You can't stay away—you must go to it."

Sol realized he was right. Things of beauty heightened the sensation when you were tapped. Tap-heads would be drawn to the geysers like flies to a light.

"Do you know what happens to a human when exposed to those fumes?" continued Karlson. "Your flesh hardens. Like rock."

Sol glanced over at the figures in the garden. *What...?*

"And the color your skin turns is unpredictable. It depends on your blood type."

"But... but..." sputtered Sol. "The masks. The filter masks."

"You asshole! Do you think a tap-head has the sense to put on a mask? Or if he did, to check to see if the filter's used up?"

Oh, god. Oh, my god!

"Yes, my friend. You should always check your filter. It should be white, like this," Karlson pointed to his own face. "If it's green, you're dead."

Sol raised a shaky hand to his face and gently removed his filter from its pouch. He stared down in horror at the bright green wafer that he held in his hand. He was stunned for a few seconds. Then...

"You bastard!" Sol lunged at Karlson. "Give me a filter, you old..."

Sol stopped in his tracks as Karlson pulled out a small weapon from a pocket in his suit. It was an outdated hand weapon, almost an antique. But it was powerful enough to vaporize Sol where he stood.

"Rule number one out on the Syr," yelled Karlson, "never give up your only filter."

Sol's eyes rolled in his head, searching around in panic. He spun around, looking back towards the shack.

"Don't bother, my friend. You won't find any filters back there."

"Christ, man. I can't believe you're doing this just because some of your Mironite friends went crazy and got themselves gassed."

"Who said it was just *some* of them?"

Sol's mind raced. What to do? The city! Karlson said the city was safe.

Sol checked out the oncoming geysers. The noise was unbearable now. The sound was like a thunderous waterfall punctuated by a pummeling boom-boom as geyser after geyser erupted. Some of the geysers were within a hundred meters. They were so close that the two men were being showered with debris thrown up by the plumes. But so far no geysers had appeared in the area between the garden and the city.

I can make it! Just gotta run for it.

Sol ran off as fast as he could. He guessed, correctly, that Karlson wouldn't shoot him in the back.

It was hard to run with the ground heaving below him. He panted heavily as he labored to move his heavier-than-normal bulk.

He was about halfway there.

I'm gonna make it.

Suddenly, off to his left two geysers erupted less than 30 meters away. The blast almost knocked him off his feet. As he staggered he was buffeted by another explosion just to his right.

Oh, shit! Oh...

Sol had no time to scream before a geyser blew his body apart, tossing the pieces high into the air along with the other debris.

"Of course, most of them just got blown up," muttered Karlson.

Karlson wandered back through his garden, seeking solace amongst the figures. He had lied to Sol—he *did* get lonely out here now. More than anything he grieved over the fact that he did not get to place his son here. But Karlson was certainly glad that he didn't have to put Sol in his garden.

Besides, he had no rubies left.

To See the Long Silent Statues Leave

See the long silent statues leave
Long gone souls,
Now where the Albion arms do seek
No figures of an eminent past
Where the long view,
The long distant view,
Brings into sight the ancient shore
Where long silent statues stand
That will take you down to the forest glen
To sit with the ancient statues there
Long silent, now and then.

— William R. Ford, Jr.

VIRTUALLY YOURS

By Nina Munteanu

Vincent yanked the V-set off his head and found himself back in his apartment, lying alone and spent on his king-size bed. The cozy cabin with the fireplace had vanished. Katherine was gone.

He stared at the V-set. His vehicle to paradise. To Katherine.

Her scent of lilac lingered in his mind as he summoned her beautiful face, smiling just for him. No, he reminded himself. Not for me. For Jake, my carrier. It was Jake she smiled at. Jake she had just made love to. Jake, who smelled her desire, felt the tender stroke of her slender legs. Vincent was just along for the ride.

His eyes swept down his deformed and gnarled body. Angry boils and scars encrusted his livid hairless skin. He remembered colliding two days ago with her in a Samson Corporation hallway and her hand had unintentionally brushed his thigh. She'd jerked back, blushing with the shame of not knowing how to avoid staring at him in revulsion. Then she'd rushed off before he had a chance to speak. Probably to wash her hand. I'm just another anonymous Corporation Overseer, he thought. A nameless ugly gnome. She doesn't know that I'm Vincent, *her* Overseer, with whom she shares beautiful thoughts of life and poetry over the V-screen.

Two weeks ago she'd boldly begun to offer a few friendly comments at the end of her progress memo. He'd responded with his own and found himself looking forward to her messages more than anything else during the workday. When he opened them, he clicked straight to her post-script, leaving her formal report for later. He recalled the message she'd sent him last week that had started everything:

"Do you like poetry, Overseer? It is one of my passions. I've read a lot of Milton lately. Granted his writing is over 400 years old, yet he evokes in my soul a yearning for Eden. Do you think Eden can exist on Earth? Perhaps it is our destiny to long for it."

Up to then she'd used her worker code-name as salutation:

"Cheers, V-screen USER 134872". This time she'd signed, "Virtually yours, Katherine."

It was as he reread her signature over and over, that he'd come up with his ingenious scheme to track her down among the hundred roaming workers in the Samson Corporation research lab by assigning a carrier to work with her. It had started out innocently enough. He'd only wanted to know what she looked like. It was SenTech's fault.

His SenTech holo program and the V-set's link to a sensor embedded in Jake's forehead gave Vincent the next best thing to having Katherine. Thanks to Jake, who didn't even know he was providing Vincent this service, SenTech permitted Vincent to see, hear, feel and taste Katherine using Jake's senses. Jake had no idea of Vincent's access to the implant or that Overseers typically used them to spy on their carriers. Jake only knew that the implant provided him with enhanced cognitive abilities. Being connected directly to the central computer database was a great advantage to him in his work as Vincent's data manager.

Hoping to make the meeting pleasant for her, as well as for himself, he'd selected Jake as his carrier based on what he'd ascertained of Katherine's physical tastes in men. But once he saw her blush with desire at Jake's perfect physique, smelled her hunger, and felt Jake's heart throb, he knew that he'd wanted more all along. This would be a good ride, he'd thought, and immediately prepared his AIs for full surveillance. Jake moved fast. Following their initial inflamed encounter at Samson Corp, Jake enticed her to his secluded cabin, where he seduced her. Vincent was unprepared for the sweetness of it and how it inflamed his own forgotten desires. Through Jake, Vincent felt like a consummate lover, drawing her out patiently, using gentle, tender strokes at first then matching her escalating rhythm. She was shy though not coy and wonderfully responsive. When the lovemaking had ended, Vincent felt strange, as though he'd betrayed himself. Moved by the experience, he'd wrenched off his V-set and wrote her an E-note as her anonymous Overseer. He'd heavily quoted Milton.

"She'd never look at me the way she looks at Jake," Vincent said, glancing down at his misshapen body. Mildred, his model 20

AI droid, glided to the bed and touched his shoulder. It said in a tinny voice, "She does not know you are her Overseer, Vincent? Perhaps you should tell her, she might like you—"

"No, Mildred," he snapped. He imagined compassion in Mildred's round green eyes and let his voice soften, "She might like communicating with me as her anonymous Overseer, but I'm afraid this is the only way she'll ever look at me *that* way." He placed the V-set on the nightstand. "She could never love *me*." Vincent let out a long breath and stroked the V-set. "But I'm content with what I have." A wry smile crossed his lips as he wrestled with a pleasure edged in guilt. His creative use of SenTech's surveillance capabilities definitely stretched its intended use. "Does that make me some sort of pimp?" He eyed the folds in the sheets then stroked the sheet. Resting his gaze on the leopard-skin of his hand, he murmured, "So be it. At least I'm a harmless one."

"The library inquires as to whether you wish to save this SenTech scenario as Katherine 1 for later use?" Mildred rasped.

"Yes, yes," he said impatiently. He brought the sheet to his face, wanting to savor her scent, knowing he would smell nothing, and clenched the fabric into a ball. With a cursory glance down at his gnarled body, he jerked to his feet. "Save it."

* * *

"He's so damn ugly. Like some monster from a bad movie," Fanny whispered to Katherine as they looked for free workstations two weeks later. Fanny stared through the transparent panel to a hunched figure in the office perched above them. He was one of twenty Overseers in the Research Department of Samson Corporation, but Katherine knew which one Fanny meant. There was only one ugly Overseer.

She stole a glance up to where he paced like a feral cat, eyes flashing at them. She felt her face heat. Embarrassed for him, she quickly looked away. Of course he hadn't heard Fanny. But surely he knew what they all said about him. Could read it in their churlish glances and smirks. The glabrous skin of his face and head looked like melted wax. Its smooth surface was blemished with islands of angry bubbles and crevasses that resembled burning lava. She couldn't help thinking of the rumor that he'd actually caused the fire, which had nearly taken his life and killed several people. They'd been experimenting with a new product at the lab. The explosion took his three colleagues, including his fiancée.

"You wonder why he doesn't get some major surgery done," Fanny continued as they claimed two unoccupied workstations. "In this day and age, when nanoreconstruction's so attainable, it's as if he wants to look that way, to scare us all."

Punishing himself, Katherine thought, and felt her eyes sting. If Fanny could only look beyond his ugly shell into those eyes of gentle sadness and vulnerability. She remembered when they'd bumped into one another three weeks ago in the hallway and her hand had accidentally touched his thigh. He smelled of smoke and metal. Their eyes met and she blushed like a teenager. He had the eyes of a poet. She'd turned away without a word and fled. He'd probably thought her rude.

"Fanny, he's probably a G-type," Katherine said, glaring into space. She yanked at her chair and let herself drop into it. "G-types can't handle the side effects of nanoconstruction." Her fingers slid furiously along the alpha console, activating her virtual support and accessing the network with her code. Instantly, her station housed itself with a set of files, a virtual bookshelf filled with books, and a vase with flowers.

"Okay," Fanny said, settling into the chair next to her. She activated her virtual support: stacks of files with documents and papers and a poster of a naked man. "You don't have to get snippy about it. You'd think you liked him or something." She gazed into the distance. "I'm glad we don't know who our Overseers are—or they us. I'd die if he turned out to be mine. Imagine if he was *your* Overseer, Katherine! How awful! What irony: beauty and the beast. It's like he knows it too, knows how absurd that would be—never looks at you."

Katherine felt her face crimson. Or was it that he detested physical beauty? Found her reprehensible.

Fanny leaned into her and cocked her head. "He might as well be an AI 20, alone up there in his ivory tower, anonymously giving orders to some of us peons. Ugly as sin and cold as metal."

Katherine recoiled. "Fanny!" She focused on her computer

screen, surprised at the yearning that stirred inside her. He wasn't a machine. More like a wounded animal. No one knew the name much less the identity of his or her Overseer. But when she'd defied protocol two weeks ago and signed with her name, Katherine, he'd followed suit with his: Vincent. She knew Vincent was the beast. Felt it in her heart. Vincent's "voice" and the beast's eyes spoke the same truth. But where the ignoble beast howled baleful regrets to the moon, this beast quoted poetry to her.

No, not to *her*, she corrected herself. She was just another rude employee who bumped into him once. He didn't know she was V-screen USER 134872—now Katherine—who sent him progress memos and lately shared her personal thoughts with him. She clicked on her saved messages and found the one she was looking for, Vincent's response three weeks ago to her silly remark about poetry and Milton.

She'd reread it several times and every time her heart flipped when he used her name:

"I admire your passion for poetry, Katherine. Does it not strip prose to the very essence of what drives our soul? If you believe in destiny, then each of us is already a story waiting to be written; mine would be a tragedy. Alas, my burning desire for knowledge destroyed the thing I most loved. I do not expect to find Eden in my lifetime here on this Earth, or elsewhere, for that matter.

"You have made me curious to read Milton. His poetry remains relevant to this day. Perhaps you are right about our longing for Eden: *'These lull'd by Nightingale embracing slept, and on their naked limbs the flow'ry roof show'r'd roses, which the morn repair'd'.'*"

Following her lead, he'd signed "Virtually yours, Vincent."

Three weeks later they were still sharing personal philosophies and always found an opportunity to quote Milton.

"Now, that's more like it!" Fanny's strident voice cut into her silent rapture. Katherine jumped in her seat, swept the screen clear and looked up, face burning in anticipation of finding Fanny looking over her shoulder. But Fanny was gazing at a man striding toward them. Katherine sighed and felt a surge of pleasure. Jake. She'd met him just over two weeks ago, when Vincent had assigned them a joint task.

"Now there's a specimen." Fanny said. "What a perfect body and face. Bet he's a great lay."

Katherine blushed. She appraised Jake's showman's eyes, firm jaw that easily supported the loose smile he always wore, and a seamless brow partially hidden beneath thick curls of chestnut hair. Yes, he was a knockout. And exciting.

"You're a lucky girl." Fanny sighed.

"Yeah," Katherine said, sensing her own hesitation. "Lucky." Although they'd been physically intimate many times already, she still didn't know Jake. His charm and humor masked a reserve of quiet depth—or nothing? Could he sustain a loving relationship with her or was Jake just lustfully infatuated with her?

"He's a carrier, isn't he?"

Katherine nodded. "Carries a piece of the V-net inside him."

"That's why he's so swift and enlightened."

Katherine nodded. She didn't consider Jake exactly enlightened. Swift, perhaps. He'd managed to get her in a prone position the first day they met and every day after that.

"You're so lucky, Katherine. You've got it all."

Katherine swallowed. She'd been considering breaking off. Jake seemed more interested in using his mouth for kissing than for talking. After two weeks of wonderful sex, she began to long for the serenity that came with sharing an ordinary life with another person. She and Jake didn't seem to have much in common. They'd never conversed like she and Vincent had on the V-screen. Jake was a bored realist. And he took no interest in poetry. She resolved to break off, before he dumped her for another lustful jaunt.

"Hi, girls." Jake tussled Fanny's mop then glided to Katherine like a panther. Gathering her long hair back with both hands, he bent to kiss her on the neck. Her decision blurred at his seductive touch. Jake seized her hands and coaxed her up from her seat. "Come." He grinned like a boy hiding a lizard in his pocket. "I have something to tell you." He led her away from the workstations toward the lounge.

"What is it, Jake?" Her eyes darted around her and she looked annoyed at him. "People are watching."

"I can't tell you here. Tonight. Meet me at Samson Square, Level 2 at 23:00. That's when my evening shift ends. Promise?"

"Okay." She looked down, wondering how she was going to break the news to him.

* * *

"I love you," he said, pulling her toward him. "Marry me."

Her throat swelled. Was that his news? She had come to tell him she didn't love him, she was in love with another man. A poet.

"I need to tell you something, Jake."

"Later, later," he whispered in her hair, pulling her into an alcove of an abandoned shop. "First *my* conversation." He caressed her ear with his lips and played them over her neck and face. It sent a shiver through her. She closed her eyes and thought of Vincent: *'with thee conversing I forget all time'*. She let him maneuver her to a dark corner. He kissed her eyelids, her cheeks, her hair. Perhaps she'd been too harsh. He wanted to marry her, after all, to share an ordinary life together.

She helped him shrug out of his clothes and smelled his longing. She let him undress her, pull her down on top of him, taste the hollow of her shoulder, her breasts, her nipples. She imagined Vincent's trembling hands, his tender glance. His fingers exploring, diving into her dark longing for him. She shuddered, surrendering to her passion. *'Flesh of flesh, bone of my bone thy art'*. Later, she thought. Then thought no longer.

* * *

Something nudged Vincent awake. "Katherine is with her lover," said Mildred, peering down at him.

Vincent roused himself, wiped the sleep from his eyes and croaked, "Library, connect with SenTech sensor, subject carrier Jake. On screen." Katherine's face appeared on the huge screen on the far wall. She looked straight at him with longing. Her lips parted as she drew closer. Vincent flung off the covers and sat up, naked, ignoring his misshapen leopard-body. He snatched the V-set from the nightstand and pulled it over his head, letting the translucent screen cover his face. "Library, activate SenTech virtual program. Save this scenario as Katherine 17. Remember to voice-over 'Jake' with 'Vincent'."

The room disappeared, replaced by a dark corridor. He lay on the cold surface of the grimy floor. Her warm body slid over him and he smelled the sweet spice of her desire. Perhaps he could find Eden on Earth after all! He felt himself firm and whispered, *"Part of my soul I seek thee, Katherine, and claim my other half."*

She drew back and peered at him with wide eyes. Then she tilted her head, gave him a searching look, and leaned forward. He felt her breath on him. "Vincent?"

His heart soared. *"'How can I live without thee, how forgo thy sweet converse and love so dearly join 'd, to live again in these wild woods forlorn'?"*

She stared at him in astonishment, then broke into a wonderful smile and kissed him. She whispered into his hair, *"'With that thy gentle hand seiz'd mine, Vincent, I yielded, and from that time see how beauty is excell'd by manly grace and wisdom, which alone is truly fair'."*

Frantic for her, he clasped her and thrust into her moist haven. She gasped. "Oh, Vincent! Vincent!"

His spirit soared like a falcon to her tender loving. When it was over she leaned her cheek against his and murmured, "I love you, Vincent." He closed his eyes. If this were only true, he thought. It felt so real. When he opened his eyes she was staring at him with intense wonder. "You're crying..."

Vincent wrenched off the V-set and blinked the tears from his eyes. The room returned. He was back on his bed. The screen was dark and she was gone. Vincent glanced down at himself, covered in his own semen. He let his eyes flutter shut and clung to her sweet words of love, ignoring what he knew—that her uttering his name was the computer's doing—and imagined the sweet perfume of her love mingled in his own.

Then he bowed his head and stared at his shriveled hands. They looked like withered twigs, infested with parasites. His body a hideous monstrosity. It was obvious that she loved Jake. How could he ever think she loved him?

He swallowed down his emotion and stumbled to his feet. Clearing his throat, he said, "Please clean up the bed, Mildred. I'll be in the shower."

"Do you wish to save this scenario?" he heard its tinny voice behind him.

"Yes, yes," he growled. This was the only way he could have her. "Tell the library to flag this one with four stars."

Vincent caught his own reflection in the hall mirror and stopped. The stretched skin of his face glistened like plastic that had been meddled with, its integrity destroyed. He pulled at the single tuft of hair on his mottled head and, feeling the pain, stared into his own narrowed eyes in challenge.

The crying, the poetry, were surely *his* feelings and thoughts, not Jake's? Yet Jake had expressed them to Katherine. Up to now Vincent had been convinced that SenTech provided strictly a one-way conduit from carrier to Overseer. SenTech was designed to help Vincent sense everything that occurred to his carrier, but only as an active spectator. What just happened with Katherine implied that Jake had acted on a subliminal message from Vincent. That he, Vincent, *had initiated action.* He blinked at the realization and saw his eyes widen with excitement, then guilt and dread.

What have I started?

* * *

Katherine lay upon Jake, her cheek pressed against his furry chest. She gently stroked his hair. "You were so sweet to quote Milton," she said. "I had no idea you'd taken an interest."

Jake brushed his eyes with his hand and looked baffled. "I'm not sure why—how. It just came out of my mouth. I've never read Milton. You're the one who reads that stuff."

Her lips curled in sudden amusement. She liked seeing him vulnerable. "Perhaps a poetic muse has invaded your mind," she teased and ran her fingers through his curls. He'd shown that beneath his reserve there lay a depth she'd never suspected.

He thought for a moment. "Perhaps I should start reading it."

She buried her nose in his hair, inhaling his musky smell. "And, the crying—"

He drew back, embarrassed, and shot her a dark look. "Why did you call me Vincent? Who's Vincent?"

"Did I?" Katherine swallowed. When they'd made love, she'd lost herself in his eyes, imagined for a brief moment that he really was Vincent. Spirit and flesh mingled into one whole. She bowed her head. "He's only a character in a virtual game I was playing," she said casually. Vincent could never be really hers. Uncomfortable with her outer beauty, he'd irrevocably isolated his physical self from her. Didn't want her. She'd been sharing "love-notes" with a phantom. But Jake was physically here with her. She could touch him. Could feel his warm breath upon her face.

And he loved her. She knew that now: no one had ever wept for her before. He'd even quoted poetry to her. She decided against breaking off. Maybe there was a little of Vincent even in Jake.

Computer Age

My brain functions quicker,
smarter, outside my head.
My body works harder, longer,
when it's not me wearing it.
My fingers caress the button,
then press a better heart in motion.
My life now is just me
logging on,
accessing the monitor
of my superior self.
It greets me
like I'm nothing but
a reflection in its mirror.

— John Grey

About the Authors

M. L. ARCHER spent her childhood in the primitive remoteness of northern Idaho, then moved to near San Francisco, where she participates in the literary community. She taught "Writing for Publication" and does consulting on creative writing. Her work has been published in such diverse markets as *Trucker's Digest, Writer's Digest, The Roswell Literary Journal, Möbius,* and many others. She is also author of the novel, "The Young Boys Gone."

MARK ANTHONY BRENNAN'S work has been featured in such publications as *Challenging Destiny, On Spec, Foxfire* and *Waxing and Waning.* You can also find his work in issue 13 of *Hadrosaur Tales.* Brennan is currently the fiction editor at *Sintrigue,* a new on-line magazine of fantasy fiction. His story, "Garden of Syr" was inspired partly by frustrated attempts to make things happen in the back garden. So far the experience only conjures up revenge stories involving weeds and slugs. Brennan currently lives in Comox, on Vancouver Island.

GARY EVERY'S career has followed many diverse paths including geology, exploration, carpenter, chef, piano player, ditch digger, photographer, freelance writer, dishwasher, soccer coach, and he is currently the bonfire storyteller at Miraval Resort and Spa in Catalina, Arizona.

WILLIAM R. FORD, JR is a frequent contributor to *Hadrosaur Tales.* He lives in Lansing, Michigan and is a talented prose writer and poet.

KEN GOLDMAN was previously a high school English and Film Studies teacher (Horror and Science Fiction in Film and Literature) at George Washington High School in Philadelphia, Pennsylvania. He is a member of the Horror Writers Association. He has had stories published in *The Edge, Not One of Us, Darkness Within,* and *Hadrosaur Tales* among many others. He has received numerous awards for his writing including Second place in The Rod

Serling Memorial Foundation's 2nd Annual Writing Contest and Honorable Mentions in the Ellen Datlow and Terri Windling's *The Year's Best Fantasy and Horror Collections* in 1993 and 1995.

JOHN GREY'S work has appeared in *Weird Tales, Nebula 2000, South Carolina Review* and *English Journal*. His work has also appeared in issues 11 and 14 of *Hadrosaur Tales*. He lives in Rhode Island.

K. S. HARDY has a degree in English from Defiance College. His fantasy poetry has appeared in *Thin Ice, Wicked Mystic, Talebones, Rictus, Deathrealm, Midnight Zoo, Elegia, Black Lotus, Chasum,* and *The Black Lily*. He is a frequent contributor to *Hadrosaur Tales*. His poem, "A Plague of Birds" received honorable mention in the eleventh annual *Best of Fantasy and Horror* anthology.

JUSTIN R. LAWFER is currently a student at Edgewood College in Madison, WI. His work has appeared on the websites www.palaceofreason.com, www.pegasusonline.com, www.planetmag.com, www.Spacerat.co.uk, and http://dragonlaugh.freeyellow.com, and has been accepted by the print magazine *The Unknown Writer*. This is Justin's first appearance in *Hadrosaur Tales*. He is a fan of giant monster movies, Monty Python, and fantasy stories.

DANIEL J. LESCO has just started writing after a long and very enjoyable career as a research engineer with NASA. "The Teak Man" is his first published fiction. He lives in Ohio and is left-handed.

NINA MUNTEANU lives with her family in Ladner, British Columbia, Canada. Her nonfiction has appeared in Beautiful BC Traveller, Pacific Yachting, Shared Vision, and Cats Magazine, among others. One of her fiction stories, "Angel of Chaos" was a finalist in the Science Fiction Writers of Earth 2001 contest. It is an excerpt of a speculative novel of the same name she has just completed.

KENNETH O'KEEFE lives and writes in Pittsburgh, Pennsylvania.

CHARLES P. RIES lives and writes in Milwaukee, Wisconsin. He is currently working on a biographical memoir entitled *Riesville* about his surviving Catholicism while being raised on a mink farm in Southeastern Wisconsin. His first book of poetry entitled *bad monk: neither here nor there* was published in January 2001. His poetry and short stories have appeared in a number of publications including *Anthology, Write On!!!, Starry Night Review,* and *Ragtime Joe's Review.*

DAVID B. RILEY'S work first appeared on the pages of *Hadrosaur Tales* back in issue Number 2. He has also been published in such markets as *The Vampire's Crypt* and *Weird Stories.* He was editor of Stray Dog Press, which published the magazine *Trails: Stories of the Old West.*

SHEILA B. ROARK is a former New Yorker who lives in Euless, Texas with her husband Gail. She has been writing poetry for over 25 years. This award-winning poet's work has appeared in more than 700 anthologies and 750 literary magazines including *True Confessions, Scroll Magazine, Simply Words, Twilight Endings, The Storyteller* and *Black Creek Review* to name a few. To her, poetry is the most perfect form of communication and writing has become a driving force in her life.

Born in a barn, GEOFF SAWERS has been burgled so often he has taken to living at other people's houses most of the time, because they usually have all his stuff. He has had five books published by Two Rivers Press in England (see http://www.tworiverspress.com for details).

CHRISTINA SNG is from Singapore. Her poems have previously appeared in *Dreams and Nightmares, Flesh & Blood, Frisson, Roadworks, Space & Time,* and *Voyage Magazine.*

DONALD SULLIVAN'S short fiction has appeared in *Calliope, Alien Worlds, Detective Mystery Magazine,* and other markets.

Subscribe to *Hadrosaur Tales!*

You've read an issue and now you've decided you want a subscription to *Hadrosaur Tales*... However, you don't want to miss out on all those great back issues and wish you could have had a subscription from the beginning. Well, no need to worry, you can start your subscription from the issue you want and get great discounts!! Just specify the issue you want to start with (sorry, issues 1,4,8, and 9 are sold out.) and the number of issues you want. There are 3 issues per year.

Our vision is to bring our readers the finest literary speculative fiction and poetry. Your questions and comments are welcome and encouraged.

Start my subscription with issue #_____
(If no issue is specified, your subscription will begin with the current issue.)

Amount Enclosed

Single sample issue - $6.95	$_____
3 issue subscription - $16.50	$_____
6 issue subscription - $28.50	$_____
9 issue subscription - $40.00	$_____

Please make checks payable to "Hadrosaur Productions." All amounts are in U.S. Dollars. All prices above include shipping.

Name:_____

Address:_____

City:_____State_____Zip_____

Don't wanna cut up your issue — That's fine too. Just send us the info requested above on a sheet of paper along with your payment and we'll be happy to get your subscription going.

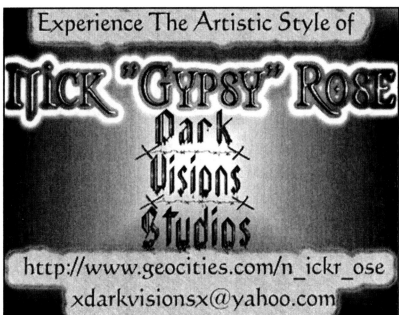